SPINE-CHILLERS

SOUTH EAST SPOOKS

Edited by Sarah Washer

First published in Great Britain in 2016 by:

 Young**Writers**

Remus House
Coltsfoot Drive
Peterborough
PE2 9BF
Telephone: 01733 890066
Website: www.youngwriters.co.uk
All Rights Reserved
Book Design by Ashley Janson
© Copyright Contributors 2016
SB ISBN 978-1-78624-159-7

Printed and bound in the UK by BookPrintingUK
Website: www.bookprintinguk.com

FOREWORD

Enter, Reader, if you dare...

For as long as there have been stories there have been ghost stories. Writers have been trying scare their readers for centuries using just the power of their imagination. For Young Writers' latest competition Spine-Chillers we asked students to come up with their own spooky tales, but with the tricky twist of using just 100 words!

They rose to the challenge magnificently and this resulting collection of haunting tales will certainly give you the creeps! From friendly ghosts and Halloween adventures to the gruesome and macabre, the young writers in this anthology showcase their creative writing talents.

Here at Young Writers our aim is to encourage creativity and to inspire a love of the written word, so it's great to get such an amazing response, with some absolutely fantastic stories. We will now choose the top 5 authors across the competition, who will each win a Kindle Fire.

I'd like to congratulate all the young authors in *Spine-Chillers - South East Spooks* - I hope this inspires them to continue with their creative writing. And who knows, maybe we'll be seeing their names alongside Stephen King on the best seller lists in the future...

Jenni Bannister

Editorial Manager

CONTENTS

Nimofe Wilson-Adu (13) 1
Swetha Lakshminarayanan 1
Anisah Isbag 2
Saakshi Panda (11).............................2
Saalihah Husain (14) 3
Abigail Ives (14) 3
Nusrath Jahan (15)..............................4
Summer Jennings (14) 4
James Morley (14)...............................5
Susannah Grace Ames (14).................5
Hridayesh Borra 6

Beechwood School, Slough

Samee Dar (13) 6
Parveer Bhachu (15) 7
Chloe Jean Miller (13) 7
Brandon Gulliford (14) 8
Lauren Barton (12) 8
Daniel West (13) 9
Sofia Khan (13)...................................9
Rachel Dunster...................................10
Layla Flemington (12) 10
Millie Mae Healy (14) 11
Ameir Said (15)..................................11
Luke Clark (12) 12
Sameer Gayum (12) 12
Hisham Ahmed 13
Nikita Santucci (13) 13
Bhavya Prashar (14)...........................14
Jack Forster (13).................................14
Fatihme Maarawi (14).........................15
Maria Gafar (14).................................15
Joshua Kurton (13) 16
Dean Murtaza (14) 16

Charles Darwin School, Westerham

Hannah Peters (13).............................17

Cox Green School, Maidenhead

Flora Demeter (14).............................17
Yasmin Pogson (14) 18
Francesca Di Cioccio (15)..................18
James Little (12) 19
Sonny Lloyd (11).................................19
Wardah Khan (11)..............................20
Ellis Reeve Bailey (11) 20
Rasa Karganroodi (11)........................21
Nadine Phelps (11).............................21
George Bowden (12)...........................22
Sienna Eden (11).................................22
Samantha Clarke (14) 23
Kirsten Elizabeth Franks (14) 23
Jessica Wood (14)..............................24
Alex Swaby (14)..................................24
Kaya Williams (14) 25
Ella Bampton (12) 25
Henry Greenwood (12)........................26
Erin-Alana Trotman (11)......................26
Romeo Mandizha (12) 27
Lewis Cartwright (11) 27
Jessica Colton (11).............................28
Nadia Rycabel (12).............................28
Abigail Sneddon (11)..........................29
Rebecca Brill (15) 29
Jason Sidhu (11) 30
Mason Brown (14)..............................30

Didcot Girls' School, Didcot

Ashia Hagger.....................................31
Abby Grace Santer (13) 31
Aislínn McGuigan (13)........................32
Vikky McRitchie (12) 32
Iqra Haleem.......................................33
Chloe Louise Jacobsen (12) 33
Daisy Duckham (13)...........................34

Davina Tyrrell (12) 34
Megan Potthast (12) 35
Chlöe Jennifer Chadwick (13) 35

Emperia College, Luton

Fatima Tuz-Zohra (15) 36
Umayr Zamir (12).............................36
Sumayyah Baksh (13) 37
Saira Khan (11)................................37

Gosford Hill School, Kidlington

Eve Mundy (13)................................38
Ben Hague (13) 38
Nadia Ella Rose Lowndes (13) 39
Aaron Holley (13).............................39
Ben Martin (13) 40
Jack Launchbury (13)........................40
Benjamin Male (13)...........................41
Ellie Eldridge (13) 41
Cameron Fox (13) 42
Emily Brandish (16)...........................42
Jacob Orton (13) 43
Lili Vieira (13)..................................43
Joe Otter (14) 44
Mason Smith....................................44

Heybridge Alternative Provision School, Heybridge

Maddie Kemp (13) 45

Highdown School & Sixth Form Centre, Reading

Tara Edwards (12) 45
Mikolaj Kajetan Misiewicz (13)...........46
Katie Hill (13)..................................46
Deyana Harmony McKiernan (13)......47
Ellie Drake (13) 47
Niamh Herbert (12) 48
Naomi Tappern (12) 48
Harvey Wright (12) 49
Alex Tonkin (12) 49
Alyshba Sassoon (12)........................50
Libby Louise Gutteridge (13)..............50

Rory Edwards (12) 51
Vickey Kios (12)...............................51
Binson Gurung (12)...........................52
Charlie Fuller (12) 52
Zeynah Hussain (12).........................53
Grace Douglas (12) 53

John O'Gaunt Community Technology College, Hungerford

Joe Jones (14)..................................54
Hannah Glover (13) 54
Rachel Cooper (13) 55
Phoebe Piper (13).............................55
Molly Lewis (13) 56
Georgia Smith (13)............................56
Morgan Henderson 57
Molly Munro (14) 57
Rebecca May Shailes (13) 58
Jordan Joanna Susan Mosdell (14) 58
Leon Davies (11) 59
Evie Chester (11) 59
Beth Pollard (14) 60
Ella Moyle (14)................................60
Edward Peter Hawkins (13)................61
Thomas Morgan-Matthews (12).........61
Ellie Bampton...................................62
Molly Rixon (12) 62
Aaron Lord (11)...............................63
Katherine Natton-Bell (11).................63
Chloe O'Brien (12) 64
Kerry Louise Hillier (11) 65
Theo Carreck (11) 65
Christopher Hillier (11) 66
Sam Featherstone (12).......................66
Bradley Elliott Smith (11) 67
Zoe Maidment (11) 67
Max Hunt (11)..................................68
Ellis Buju Morgan (12) 68
Corbin Swabey (12)...........................69
Daisy Lockhart..................................69
Ceara Lynne Fowkes (12) 70
Cory Hale (14).................................70

Molly-Jayne Moore (14)....................71
Ellie Griffiths (13) 71
Oren Fowkes 72
William McLaughlin (11) 72
Chloe Langford (14) 73
Ciaran Morrison (13)........................73
Alex Vasko (14) 74
Liam Benson (14) 74
George Maslin (13)...........................75
Chelsea Smith (14)...........................75
Matthew Lugg (14) 76
Georgie Prismall (11)........................76
Isabelle Barnes (11)..........................77

Kennet School, Thatcham

Jordan Luke Bartlett (17) 77
Emily Walker (17) 78
Bethany-Jo O'Neill (17) 78
Emily Thomas (16)............................79
James Elstone (16) 79
Aran Willett (16)...............................80

Loxford School of Science & Technology, Ilford

Kareena Kaur Tooray 81

Madni Institute, Slough

Faiza Waheed (13) 82
Hajira Jamil (13) 82
Zainab Ahmed (11) 83
Raiha Noor (14) 83
Maria Jabeen....................................84
Sumayya Aisha Ali (14) 84
Sara Muhammad 85
Manzil Khan (11)..............................85
Aisha Khan (14) 86
Laura Daghes (14)............................86
Laiba Qadeer (14)............................87
Maryam Rahman (12).......................87
Afiyah Ahmed (13)............................88
Sumaiyah Naz Naz Bhatti (13)...........88

Reading School, Reading

Stefan Darling (14) 89

St Bartholomew's School, Newbury

Sanskriti Sahoo (12) 89
Alex Rance (12).................................90
Frankie Lochhead (13) 90
Harry Clarkson (12)...........................91
Ellie Starling (13)..............................91

St Benedict's Catholic College, Colchester

Anna Kelpi (12) 92
Treasure Chimsom Chima (13)..........92
Frances Broatch (14)..........................93
John Lynch (15).................................93
Daryl Cother (15) 94
Dmitriy Koshonko (15) 94
Phoebe Dyball (14)...........................95
Luigi Sombilon (15) 95
Niamh O'Neill (13)............................96
Milly Thurston (12)............................96
Daniel Claxton (13)...........................97
Jessica Brown (12)............................97
Dawid Kurzawa 98
Yanira Allen-Meha (13).....................98
Beatrice Nardi (12)...........................99
Ellie-Mae Pledger (13) 99
Raymond Ese (14) 100
Joseph Guild (12)............................100
Sam Rundle (12) 101
Amber Coultrup (14) 101
Rose Jones (13)...............................102
Zoe Pearson (13).............................102
Marie Sofia Sebaratnam (14)...........103
Emily Louise Pavey (13) 103
Benita Mansi (14) 104
Delphine Masterson (13)..................104
Elizabeth Igbinoba (13)...................105
Anthony Oluwapelumi
Sanyaolu (13) 105
Bandi Cserep (12)............................106
Jamie Baker....................................106
Cieran Montgomery 107
Julian Olivagi 107

Maddie Barrell (12) 108
Tom Brown......................................108
Chenile Sulley 109
Jay Alvarez (13)..............................109
Anton Alvarez (13)...........................110
Olivia Farry (12)...............................110
Freya Richardson (12) 111
Shannon Payne 111

St Birinus School, Didcot

Joseph Edmans (12) 112
Sam Will (12)...................................112
Jack Greenaway (11)........................113
Joe Churchill Stone (11)....................113
William Marron 114
Jamie Staples (11) 114
Kian Lay (11)...................................115
Alfie Grisbrooke 115
Emmanuel (11) 116
Jamie McMenemy (12) 116
Felix Marsh 117
Casey Muldoon (11).........................117
Ethan James More O'Ferrall (13) 118
Samuel Hart (12)..............................118
Corey Swaine (12).............................119
Myles Hicks (12)...............................119
Jacob Eamonn Sykes (13) 120

St George's School, Ascot

Ruby Anna Carty-Din (12) 120

St Mark's West Essex Catholic School, Harlow

Jade Creamer 121
Lucy Denham 122
Alice Wybrew 122

Sarah Bonnell School, London

Bhavika Makwana (13) 123

Shirley High School , Croydon

Connor Gammon (12).........................123
Chloe Fillon-Payoux (13) 124
Andrew Jones (11)............................124

Curtis Peacock (12) 125
Rojon Yilmaz (12) 125
Hannah Bance (12) 126
Jacob Hue (12) 126
Abigail Asantewaa (12)....................127
William Daniels White (12)...............127
Omer Sunay Ibrahim (13) 128
Raul Perez Hernandez (12) 128
Rovita Tambwe (12) 129
Eren Aziz Aray (12) 129
Amirah Tahir (12) 130
Lauren Wills (12) 130
Shamoy Chenel Simmonds (11).......131
Leah Palmer (13) 131

The Bedford Sixth Form, Bedford

Megan Massey (16).........................132

The Urswick School, London

Melike Ozzengin (14) 132

Wallingford School, Wallingford

Molly Francesca Ferris (11)..............133

Wood Green School, Witney

Bethan Richie (12) 133
Blaine Eason (12) 134
Graeme Bateman (12)......................134
Meagan Brien (13) 135
Kayleigh Gardikioti-Griva (12).........135

THE MINI SAGAS

Death Claims You

The red blood moon hangs full in the starless sky as you enter the forbidden woods. Prowling reluctantly to the cave, where certain death awaits, you tremble as you see the bloody, mangled corpses of previous victims. You take a quick glance back, remembering your family's faces as you were chosen, mortified and mournful.

Hearing the growl, you snap your head back, coming eye to eye with the monster, the demon's eyes that shine with bloodlust and undying hunger.

Immediately, you know your fate has been sealed as it pounces and devours you. You shriek helplessly, death claims you...

Nimofe Wilson-Adu (13)

Blink

I open my eyes to the dull walls of the prison cell, peals of sardonic laughter ringing in my ears. I stare down at the lengthy knots that bind my limbs together. Escaping isn't an option. It doesn't matter – I'll be gone soon, for sure.

I turn my head to the timer, the numbers counting down, taunting me. I can hear the seconds tick by, my life slowly reaching its end. *Tick-tock, tick-tock.* In the blink of an eye, my life flashes before my eyes, childhood memories invading my consciousness. In another, the world is on fire. *Blink.*

Swetha Lakshminarayanan

Nobody Will Survive...

Like a statue, I abide. Lifeless. Frozen in thought; frozen in movement. Watching in horror as flaming red arms embrace my house in a destructive hug.

Realisation hits me... *Mum's in there!* Instinct overrides lucidity and I find myself running towards Armageddon. Clenched by a fireman's talons, I'm dragged away.

'No! My mum's in there! Please!'

Propelling myself forward, I desperately scream and resist, but to no avail.

'Stop! Your mother will get out safely!'

They were lying. Nobody would survive.

'No!' I wail as the roof collapses, validating my fears. Burning the bridge between my mother and myself.

'Mum... ?'

Anisah Isbag

Me And The Ghost

Sweat poured over me. Like a subzero river, submerging me under its powerful waves. I shuddered uncontrollably — but not due to the cold. Long, blood-red fingernails scraped noisily against my bedroom window. *Screech!* The noise sent shudders racing up and down my spine.

'Mum, Dad... ?'

I was alone. Me and the ghost.

Saakshi Panda (11)

The Creeper

Boom! Boom! Boom!
Three gunshots, three dead people.
I ran. My heart pounding, my breath ragged. I ran, turning right and left, going round and round, never finding the path to survival. With every wrong turn, my mind was growing crazier.
Boom! Boom!
They were hot on my tail.
Adrenaline coursing through my veins, I sprinted towards the exit blindly, my lungs blazing with fire. Before I could react, it leapt into my path. Rosy-red blood all over its pale skin, eyes bloodshot and hungry, its back hunched, ready for prey.
My life was over before it had begun.

Saalihah Husain (14)

The Note

Scrawled into the chipboard, blood dripping from the letters; it was from her. The girl from beneath. The one running, the one with red eyes, red as the crimson on a blade's edge.
The lights flickered once more and I was plunged into darkness. Breath was cracked and rigid, echoing into the night. The silence threatened by what came next.
Slowly, another line was scratched in. The clawing and scraping disturbed the silence... I wasn't alone.
Death comes to those who wait.

Abigail Ives (14)

The Unknown

Pearls of blood danced gracefully across my leg, clinging onto the flesh that was brutally torn open. A sharp pain raced through my veins, as I tore the branch away and cried out in agony. Darkness spread through the sky, eliminating the sunlight that shone down its rays of hope.

It's coming, I can feel it. Forcing myself to remain strong, I frantically dragged myself across the land. Soft growling echoed and started its crescendo. Its silent screeching pierced through my ears; a spine-chilling breeze rushed by me. Goosebumps crept up my arm as it came closer and closer...

Nusrath Jahan (15)

My Black-Eyed Demons

There's a girl who keeps me awake with her singing, melodically chanting the same story, etching the same knowledge into the same scars. She's young, but there's no innocence in her black eyes.

There's the whispers of the boy who pulls out the blade and presses it into my skin. He's the one that's killing me, yet there's no remorse in his black eyes.

There's the teasing mantra that paints over scars with lies. He's the puppet master that has me dancing on the end of his string, all of my secrets locked away in his black eyes.

Summer Jennings (14)

Blank And White

His eyes closed; the light began to slowly flood and overwhelm the room. Clenching his fists, he tried to ignore the doubts that swamped his mind like a disease. His fingers, blue and numb, trembled vigorously whilst his eyes, unblinking and vein-ridden, scurried throughout the stark white.
Breathing erratically, he lurched forward, his mind cloaked by the utter void in which he was trapped, clasping the stale, solid air.
His mind raced; he couldn't, he wouldn't, he was never supposed to know... he froze – amidst the silence from the corner of the room, there protruded a calm, consistent whistle... breathing...

James Morley (14)

Without Remorse

I have come to need the feeling of normality once again. To drift meaninglessly on the coattails of Zephyrus. To elude the fate that you have condemned me to. To feel again...
I can barely recall the sensation of warmth, for my soul is forged from ice. I yearn for the comforting embrace of a mother's arms, or that spark of excitement to flare inside of me. In short, I crave the humanity you so wrongly and cruelly tore from me. And you will pay. But not with your life. You will pay with everything that makes it worth living.

Susannah Grace Ames (14)

The House

I could hear birds singing and the sun shone next to the abandoned house.
My mum said, 'Don't go near the house, it's a bit unsafe.' But I didn't believe her, it looked fine to me.
Over the years mould grew on it and the windows were smashed.
One day, I heard noises there and I went to check on the house. I opened the rusty gate, thick fog hid the house; the night sky almost made it camouflaged. It looked terrifying. I started to see shadows, then blood dripped around me.
The next day, I was in hospital.

Hridayesh Borra

The Woman In Black

John never paid much attention to the neighbours living on his city block until the day the middle-aged widow moved in two doors down. She was plump, had dull eyes and wore black gloves on her hands, even indoors.
One night, John heard screeching noises from the house, then the noise stopped. Everything fell dead silent. He turned to go back home, but there he was – trapped by the woman in black.

Samee Dar (13)
Beechwood School, Slough

The Spine-Chilling House

The house... dark, gloomy and mysterious.

There was a spooky house that no one dared enter. The moon shone, highlighting the house. A *No Trespassing* sign was shaking against the rusty and red gates. The breeze opened the gates, the broken senescent and ancient trees glanced over the spine-chilling house. The wind howled as the Gothic ghost trespassed by the hair-raising house.

The darkness took over the light, the thunder struck over the haunted house. The house was as dark as a hole of coal. The darkness crept out through the cracked window...

Parveer Bhachu (15)
Beechwood School, Slough

Untitled

One night, a family settles down, watching a TV drama series, 'Scream'. They don't realise the danger that will occur that night.

The phone rings and the mother gently answers. All she hears is, '*Do you and your husband want to die tonight, because your child surely didn't.*'

The mother, panicking, answers, 'Don't be so silly, my child is sat right here, next to me.'

A shadow exits the room. Swiftly, the mother turns to her child worriedly, to see her child's neck slit open.

The family is never seen again.

Chloe Jean Miller (13)
Beechwood School, Slough

Possession

I felt the pressure on my back, somewhere between awake and a dream. I lay helpless, motionless, screaming in my mind, fighting with the rebellion of a stallion. It had pinned me down, so cold and pushing into my lungs. Heavy, menacing, it was penetrating my core. It high C-pitched screeching burning my ears, mocking me, wild with pleasurable Satanic desire.

Then, it happened, nothing, emptiness so wide it made it hurt to breathe. Or perhaps it was the thing inside me. My soul, my essence was crushed into a corner, silenced by what took over.

Brandon Gulliford (14)
Beechwood School, Slough

Mystery Person

There was a girl who went into the dim park on her own. Some aggressive kids came and killed her, nobody knew what happened. Even though she is dead, she swings herself with her head tilted. She only kills children, she does not know who killed her.

When she was being killed, she saw that his person had a school uniform on. She had black, bloody hair, black devil eyes and a school uniform on.

It only took a minute before her murderer came back and there in front of her was the murderer...

Lauren Barton (12)
Beechwood School, Slough

The Night

As night fell, the wind howled. Jody was asleep, but there was a sudden knock on her door. She crept downstairs and all she could hear was a little child's giggle.

When she got downstairs, the flame of a dragon roared. She saw her lounge door and opened it. There it was. A girl was sitting there in the corner of the room, crying. Jody crept over towards the girl, the girl heard her presence and screamed! Jody turned and the girl vanished. Was it her imagination, or was there really a ghost?

Daniel West (13)
Beechwood School, Slough

In The Dark

In the dark, the monsters lurk...

Jasmine, Zack, Dean and I were chosen for a trust exercise. We arrived at the forest, we walked. Night fell quickly, we made a fire and got our sleeping bags ready. Slowly, my eyes felt heavy and I fell asleep.

'Wake up!' Zack nudged me.

'What do you want?' I screamed, I was so tired.

'Jasmine and Dean are gone,' he told me.

We got our torches and saw... bodies, with crimson blood dripping down like a waterfall. *They bled to death,* I thought.

Something emerged from the dark... 'Help me!'

Sofia Khan (13)
Beechwood School, Slough

What's That?

One day, there was a girl called Mather. She was just like any ordinary teenager. She didn't listen to her parents and just did what she wanted. This was going to haunt her.

She was strolling in the woods, when all of a sudden she felt she was being watched. She ran as fast as she could to her mum's house, but what she saw was her mum, lying on the floor, dead.

Suddenly, she heard the door lock all by itself. In crept a man-shaped figure and that would be the last thing she would ever see.

Rachel Dunster
Beechwood School, Slough

Demon Teacher!

Mr Alucard was a teacher at Swampville High. By day he was an ordinary teacher, but by night he became Dracula.

During his lessons there was always one student messing around, he didn't say anything, just gave him the evil eye. Unexpectedly, Mr Alucard came to Jonathan's house.

Jonathan heard a gentle tap on his window. He faced the window, there he was – Mr Alucard, smiling menacingly. Jonathan froze in fear. He ran downstairs as fast as he could, it was too late... Mr Alucard was already there.

'Mr A-Alucard!' Jonathan said, trembling with fear.

'It's Dracula!'

Jonathan was gone!

Layla Flemington (12)
Beechwood School, Slough

Never Underestimate

The oak door shudders under my hand. *Stop it,* I tell myself - doors don't shudder. I peer round the edge before I can stop myself and immediately regret it. He isn't there.

I will kill him; kill him for Clara. My Clara.

I found her corpse in three separate pieces. Resentment burns like a wildfire attacking my body, that's why I don't feel – feel the hand grasp my neck, the knife that unleashes a crimson torrent down my front as the ground rushes towards me. He paints me with his warning for another victim, the one I ignored...

You're next.

Millie Mae Healy (14)

Beechwood School, Slough

Behind The Doors

As the night grew deeper, Freddie and Mary were knocking on doors, collecting sweets. They came across a bright door, unaware of the secrets which lay behind the door. Screams seemed part of the decoration, becoming more realistic as they were lured toward the house. They knocked, finding the door was already open. Their spirit of adventure led them to enter. Mary screamed as a glass bottle attacked her head, knocking her unconscious. The lights switched off. Where the moonlight shone through, a beastly man held a glass bottle dripping blood.

Another scream was released!

Ameir Said (15)

Beechwood School, Slough

Haunted Hotel

There is a haunted hotel with a lift. Some people get in, their names are Mr Scarred and Mr Death. They are in the lift when it stops with a bang! The lift door opens with a creak, they run out of the lift. They look around and see a zombie. They run as fast as they can, but Mr Scarred gets bitten and turns into a groaning zombie.
The place is covered in blood and guts. In the lift people are screaming. Suddenly the lift door opens, they scream again at what they see...

Luke Clark (12)
Beechwood School, Slough

The Haunted House

Zombie was late for his marriage. He stole a plane and took a short cut into the woods. His plane ran out of fuel and crash-landed in the wood.
Next to it was a big haunted house. He went in and found ghouls, ghosts, demons, werewolves and evil robots. They were all chasing him... they were shooting guns. Skeletons appeared.
Zombie won, he went back to get married.

Sameer Gayum (12)
Beechwood School, Slough

The Mysterious Forest

It was a cold and misty night in the forest. There were two people killed in the forest. A boy called Bob and a girl called Kacey. They were related.

They were walking alone with a backpack filled with water bottles, food and torches. They looked around to see if danger was approaching. Both of them were scared.

Whilst they were walking, Bob said that he was hungry and thirsty. He kneeled down to get water and food from his bag and as he turned around, Kacey was missing...

Hisham Ahmed
Beechwood School, Slough

The Figure

It was dark, my heart stopped. There, stood in front of me, was an ominous house in the darkness. Trees swaying in the wind, foreboding, alone; the shining moon watched over the abandoned house. I could feel the soggy mud soaking through my shoes. I could hear wolf howls. I could almost taste the dampness in the air. The moon was gleaming, the stars were shining, the sky as blue as the ocean.

In the distance, the figure stood. A black silhouette, nothing but its hair blowing in the wind, wearing only black, face covered. The figure remained unknown.

Nikita Santucci (13)
Beechwood School, Slough

Untitled

Jean walked towards the gates. *Creak!* The gates swung open as the wind blew, scaring the life out of her. She screamed and tried to control herself. She didn't want to get caught. Before she crept in, she looked left and right and behind her to make sure that nobody could see her and find her entering.

Although she was still scared, she walked towards the damp, smelly porch of the abandoned house. The tall trees danced as the wind blew and the leaves trembled. Slowly, the front door opened as Jean turned her head towards the creepy, abandoned house...

Bhavya Prashar (14)
Beechwood School, Slough

Untitled

One day, parents of two children went out for dinner, they hired a babysitter to look after the children.

As it got later, the babysitter put the children to bed. At about 9:30pm, the babysitter rang the parents to ask if she could watch TV, because they only had one which was in the parents' bedroom. The parents said yes, the conversation then went silent.

The babysitter said, 'Oh, before you go, please can I move the clown statue?'

Instantly, the parents shouted, 'Get out of the house, now!'

Everyone in that house died that night.

Jack Forster (13)
Beechwood School, Slough

Graveyard

The old, brown, crackly gate creaked. I walked through the old, spooky graveyard. There were strange noises and something creepy, like a ghost. Dark shadows passed, my heart started to beat faster and faster.

Eventually I saw a bright light in the distance, near a haunted house. Without warning, in the distance I saw a person walking around. Was it a person with those weird eyes? Or was it a deadly ghost with white eyes?

There were footsteps, *tip, tap*. I ran as fast as I could, but there was someone following me. I felt something catch my neck – dead!

Fatihme Maarawi (14)
Beechwood School, Slough

Life After Death

Hello, I'm writing from beyond the living. There are truly no words that can explain my state of mind. Hesitation won't make me feel any better, because the truth is that there is no surpassing the inferior. I was haunted by the guilt of my past that dispatched me slowly. I was not able to breathe, let alone live another antagonising day. The ominous power of the unknown can be diabolical. I soon had no reason to live the horrid life that I had led to oblivion. The meaningless day after day made me loathe the unforeseen.

Maria Gafar (14)
Beechwood School, Slough

Abandoned

There was an old abandoned house on the corner of the street. No one there. No light, no shadow. Could it be abandoned?
We stood and stared, it wasn't long before we went to explore. Nerves rushing up and down, head pounding. Nothing would stop me.
I grabbed the handle, my mates behind me. They heard a noise so they turned round. As they turned back to look at the door, I was gone...

Joshua Kurton (13)
Beechwood School, Slough

Lurking Hound

The dog lurked around the area with its bloodshot eyes, tongue halfway out of its mouth. He saw his next victim. Eyes locked, he ran towards it, barking as loud as he could.
He pounced on it, chewing on its neck. Blood coming through its throat. No one there but the dog and its victim.
Who is the next victim?

Dean Murtaza (14)
Beechwood School, Slough

A Strange Turn

'Bloody Mary, Bloody Mary, Bloody Mary,' I turned round three times. On the final pivot a chill ran down my spine. Nothing happened. I lingered in the bathroom for a few seconds before turning on my heel and crashing into the door. The door never used to be just behind the sink, did it? I opened it anyway and found myself, alone, in a corridor. The bell must have gone already, but I'm sure I wasn't that long. Ambling cautiously, I peered suspiciously around for a door, but there was none. Or windows, just a deserted corridor...

Hannah Peters (13)
Charles Darwin School, Westerham

The Late-Night Walk

It was two minutes past midnight, I was walking by myself. I needed to get some fresh air. I was walking past my friend's house and the school. I was walking for another five minutes when I got to an abandoned graveyard. There were no flowers or anything that showed a little bit of caring. In the dim light there was a dark silhouette of a body. I also heard footsteps. I turned around, then I saw two eyes that looked like two yellow circles.
I got scared, pretty scared. I saw someone coming up to me, I started running...

Flora Demeter (14)
Cox Green School, Maidenhead

The Care Home

The slow music filled the empty atmosphere with a meaningless Christmas song. The faces of the old people were dragged down with the bad memories engulfing their sorry brains.

'Turn that off!' A bellow came deep from within the throat of a man in the corner facing the window.

Only a few had ever witnessed him out of the dark silhouette that covered him wherever he went. But no one had ever seen him out of the chair.

Bang! The lights went out, leaving a single candle lighting the corner beside the chair. Tony had gone.

Yasmin Pogson (14)
Cox Green School, Maidenhead

The Deed

As he lay lifelessly on the cold, wooden floorboards, Lolita paced around the room, her heart pounding and mind racing; what was she going to do? His face was already discolouring to a pale snow-white. She didn't have much time.

Tugging effortlessly at the harsh, dead limbs, the sound of a roaring car engine coming to a stop disrupted her actions. She had run out of time. They were here.

Frantically pounding around the room, she covered the deceased's body with a thin blanket, concealing her secrets. There was a knock at the door, her cold, dead heart stopped...

Francesca Di Cioccio (15)
Cox Green School, Maidenhead

Death Is Upon You

The detective walked into the haunted stone cabin to find the suspect, finding a letter addressed to him, saying: *'You need to leave the man in the suit and red tie. He will kill you as soon as you read this!'*
A white, cold hand gripped his shoulder and when he looked, it was the man with a white face, suit and red tie. The detective's death was upon him.
He opened his mouth very slowly, his life was doomed. He was shaking, then the man in the suit killed him.

James Little (12)
Cox Green School, Maidenhead

The Crow

I'm on the edge of my branch, clinging on with my sharp claws. I watch as the girl keeps running, the man lurks behind her with a sinister look on his face. He's dressed in a mysterious black cape with a hood covering his face. Flapping my wings in sympathy for the girl, she screams! The tears sprint down her face, creating a puddle of despair which is drowning her.
The orphan girl runs into the church, followed by the man. I swoop inside, ripping down the hood...
A ghost! The man snatches the girl and fades slowly away.

Sonny Lloyd (11)
Cox Green School, Maidenhead

Help...

'Argh!' I screamed.
It happened again. Why? A knock came.
'Get ready to go to school,' said my mum.
Surprisingly, I was already ready. I went to have breakfast and then went to school.
'Help me! No don't... ' said a voice.
I turned around and saw mum falling, with a knife through her stomach. The man ran away. I left.
Finally I was at school...
'Hey,' said my mate.
'Hi,' I said, without looking at him. I then looked.
'Argh! Get away from me, go!' I screamed.
He looked exactly like the person I saw in my nightmare.

Wardah Khan (11)
Cox Green School, Maidenhead

The Horror Story

Crash, bang! The door fell down suddenly, I sprinted to my window, I peered outside. There was nothing except the helpless moon. I heard footsteps, I screamed in horror.
I saw the shadow of a murderous soul. The dark figure had a mysterious weapon, like a chainsaw. The man came into my room...

Ellis Reeve Bailey (11)
Cox Green School, Maidenhead

The Undead Spirit

Jess was brain-frozen after he saw his dead father behind him in his selfie. He was plodding down to his living room. Then he heard the basement door open. He entered the basement, hearing whispering. 'Remember Jess, you still don't have a job.'

He was going to explode when he heard that mumble come to his head. Then past phrases were whispering in his mind from his father, who'd passed away long ago.

Then the noises came from a cupboard. He stepped towards the cupboard, sweat was dripping from his forehead. He slowly and carefully opened the cupboard...

Rasa Karganroodi (11)
Cox Green School, Maidenhead

Where's Wolfie?

It was a dark night.

'Argh!' Wolfie screamed as a blood-dripping orange-skinned zombie came closer and closer.

Wolfie stepped back with fright. He then suddenly started to run and unexpectedly the zombie started to follow Wolfie wherever he went. Ever since then, the zombie has never left Wolfie, not even for a second.

A while after that, Wolfie was never seen again. Ever again!

Nadine Phelps (11)
Cox Green School, Maidenhead

The Unexpected Knock

One extraordinary night, a young boy named Jack had been left home alone. There had been reports showing that a ghostly figure was roaming the streets and going inside random citizens' homes. Jack had turned his TV off and gone to bed. Also he locked his door from any upcoming scares.

Fifteen minutes later, the lava lamp switched on and off. Jack gasped out loud. Smashes and bangs began to occur downstairs. Jack crept out of his room and got to the top of the stairs, as he creaked down the stairs a knock sounded.

'I've found you Jack... '

George Bowden (12)

Cox Green School, Maidenhead

The Doll With The Powers

I am three days into living in my new home. To be totally honest, I hate it.

The little girl is attached to me and she takes me everywhere. I just want to be alone. I think it's time to create some evil. This girl is going to be so surprised. My perfect plan is to sneak up on her and with my magical powers, *boom!* I will make her into a werewolf.

Sienna Eden (11)

Cox Green School, Maidenhead

The Woman

It was Tuesday when I saw her. She watched me when I came to and from school, it became a daily routine to look up at her in her ivy-infested window.

However, it was that morning, she wasn't there. I didn't think much of it as I didn't even know her. But it had been three months since the first sighting of her and it felt strange.

Later that evening, the whole neighbourhood had a power cut and I was home alone. At least I thought I was until I saw her, the woman. Thing is though – she's dead...

Samantha Clarke (14)

Cox Green School, Maidenhead

The Mango Tree

I do not perceive the darkness that has come to take me...
But then I did.

It was watching me. I ran like a deer cornered by a lion. The light had run too, off into the forest.

I ran and ran to the mango tree. Not thinking, I crashed straight into where it happened, where she was. The mango tree was ravaged with scratches. This was how she died; how I would too... I felt darkness wash over me. And I let it. I was defeated, helpless. I saw her eyes burning red.

Then it consumed me...

Kirsten Elizabeth Franks (14)

Cox Green School, Maidenhead

It's Your Turn

You said till death do us part, yet you stand there with your deceit painted on your face. You lied to me. I tried to convince myself that what I was going to do was right, but was it? My words were desperate to escape. My eyes were dead – killed by your betrayal. You played the victim yet it was me who was suffering, me that got hurt. But now it's your turn. Your turn to feel the hurt, the pain, your turn to feel the knife...

Jessica Wood (14)
Cox Green School, Maidenhead

Monday Morning Blues

I woke up this morning feeling kind of transparent; must be the Monday morning blues I guess. Slowly, I got out of my bed and had breakfast. Slowly, not caring about a thing, I inhaled my breakfast. It didn't taste right; like it went right through me. Across from me was a mirror, normally I don't take notice of it, but something was different. Anyway, I opened the bedroom door and my room-mate yelled at me. Obviously I had no idea what he was on about. I looked in the mirror hanging on the wall and saw nothing there...

Alex Swaby (14)
Cox Green School, Maidenhead

The Ghost Story

It was a normal day, suddenly I heard the front door open. I ran to my room, hid in the cupboard. I was out of breath. Who were they? Why were they in my house? I waited until there was no sound and crept down the hall. I heard someone, I ran into the closest room. Someone came in, it was a little girl. She ran away.
I ran back to my room and hid. I knocked the lamp over. Then I heard footsteps coming upstairs towards my room. I didn't know what to do, I froze in fear...

Kaya Williams (14)
Cox Green School, Maidenhead

The House

One night, when the moon was full of blood... a child was drenched and looking for shelter. The time was 11pm when she found my house. I remember this night like it was yesterday. Her warm hand as she trudged towards the dilapidated house, she noticed me, a distant shadow slowly descending towards her. Her face suddenly full of fear, she suddenly bolted towards the door with sheer determination.
That night I floated around my abode, my translucent, white skin almost glowing as I searched. My ugly, ghost-like features are a curse, I would just like a friend!

Ella Bampton (12)
Cox Green School, Maidenhead

Blood Of A Boy...

'What a lovely day,' Jay whispered to himself, 'the sun is shining, this is a beautiful meadow. Ow!'
A small, blood-red, carnivorous plant locked onto his bare ankle, instantly he started bleeding. It oozed everywhere until he was going to faint! Jay suddenly couldn't breathe and a tidal wave of blood rushed out of his mouth! He crumpled to the floor like a deflated balloon. *Pfft!* He spat out some dirt, it was sucking him down.
'No-oo,' he screamed, 'not like this!'
He hit some ground with incredible force.
'What?'
He had a weird headache... he had horns!
'What now?'

Henry Greenwood (12)
Cox Green School, Maidenhead

The Fair

'Argh,' screamed a voice.
But whose voice? Earlier that night a couple came to the fair. It was Friday the 13th and it wasn't any normal night.
As I said, they went strolling into the fair. First they went into the haunted house. That's when everyone heard the scream.
'Oh no!' screamed a woman. Then the boy came out with bloody hands.
He said, 'Who's next... ?'

Erin-Alana Trotman (11)
Cox Green School, Maidenhead

The Transformation Of Doom

As the scarlet-red moon approached, it instantly caught my eye, within seconds. I saw a shadowy figure approach me. Who was it? I slowly walked, step by step, I felt a slimy, greasy hand touch me. Then...
'Argh!'
I felt agony so painful I couldn't even imagine it. What had happened? Just then I realised... I was a horrible monster. I rapidly ran home to check in the mirror.
I was part human, part various animals. Strangely beautiful, aquatic eyes, three joined legs with a poisonous stinger! I knew the only thing was to pass it on to someone...
You!

Romeo Mandizha (12)
Cox Green School, Maidenhead

Shadow

I could see it everywhere, everywhere I went. Whether I was awake or asleep, I would always see it.
At night I always had a dream that included the shadow. If I looked forward, it would be there, if I looked back it would be there. The longer I stared at it, the closer and bigger it got.
One day, it will get me...

Lewis Cartwright (11)
Cox Green School, Maidenhead

A Twin Is Suddenly Scary!

There was once a girl called Jenny. She lived in an unusual house. It was winter, near Christmas. She went to bed one night.
Suddenly, 'Argh!' she screamed and again in horror.
There, in front of her was a creepy, spooky, zombie-like version of her. So she pinched herself to see if it was a dream. The twin bad version of her had a dagger in her hand, the normal Jenny threw a slipper at her to see if it was a ghost. Was she going to be able to stop it, or even kill it... ?

Jessica Colton (11)
Cox Green School, Maidenhead

The Mystery Of Lockwood School

It was just past twelve. The sun was shining through the translucent windows of the old science class. My hand felt underneath the wooden table, gum, sticky, revolting gum. How could this day get any more boring?
Suddenly I heard something, then a scream. Perhaps this day wouldn't be so boring. Then 'it' came. Only one strand of greasy hair sticking out from the blistered scalp. Dribble dripping from the thin lips. Eyes flickering from one light to another. Everyone was shaking and silent. It looked at me, it pointed at me.
'You!' it hissed...

Nadia Rycabel (12)
Cox Green School, Maidenhead

The Evil Crow

My black wings shadowed a young girl as I swooped down upon her. She lay down on an old, musty grave and connected her hands together to pray. It was a cold night, the wind was howling, the moon was beaming down as I savagely attacked her.
'Argh, get off me!' she screamed.
I grabbed at her black lace dress with my vicious claws. I grinned as the dust spun round in the air. I shot off in evilness and cackled in happiness. A car pulled over.
'Where are you?' shouted her mum.

Abigail Sneddon (11)
Cox Green School, Maidenhead

The Hospital

Screams of lobotomy echo through the ward. Footsteps one hopes don't stop outside your door. One for Smith, two for Simon, three for you! Counting in pairs, like the beat of drums; the battle you face is to the grave.
Silence. No it can't be. It's not your time. Blinding light floods in, basking your ghostly white skin. Guards, more like brutes, drag you to the dreaded operation chamber. Next to you, on the shiny, metallic trays lie an ice pick and a petite hammer.
'Hold him down!' Doctor Dorian calls.
Black is all that remains; nothing but black!

Rebecca Brill (15)
Cox Green School, Maidenhead

The Football Hazard!

Hazard = Footballer And Risk

Surprisingly, the red moon appeared on a Saturween night. The Chelsea team were training, captain, Sidhu was torturing Hazard. Was he okay?

Finally, Ellis and George had arrived at Stamford Bridge. They couldn't care less.

Hazard got changed, Ellis did as well. The Ellis boasted and bit Hazard. He was a cannibal.

The game had started, in the first half Chelsea were winning; then the full moon appeared. Hazard turned into a wolf-devil and soon murdered everyone.

Hazard stated, 'Who's the beast? Hazard, Hazard is!'

The full moon had passed by, Hazard turned into a vicious vampire!

Jason Sidhu (11)

Cox Green School, Maidenhead

Doge

A long time ago, in a galaxy far, far away, there was a kid who was playing Middle Earth: Half Arkham Fallout Creed, Return of the Jedi, episode one, part two, the pre-sequel, game of the year edition 2012. He had a dog named Doge who was spooky, very spooky.

One day Doge mauled and ate the kid. Also the kid's mum and dad. It was very, very scary.

Nobody lived, everyone died by the dog's paw. It was terrifying, very terrifying.

Mason Brown (14)

Cox Green School, Maidenhead

The Deadly Doll

There was a harsh knock at the front door, who could it be at this time of night? Hesitantly, I opened the door and at my feet was a peculiar-looking willow basket. There was an unsettling giggle coming from within. Looking down, I saw a blonde-haired doll. Cautiously bringing it inside, I wondered why it was left at my door.

Suddenly, the lights blew out, all I could see was a flickering candle and a silhouette in my peripheral vision. Slowly, I turned around. Next to the candle stood a small figure gripping a poised knife; I had no escape.

Ashia Hagger
Didcot Girls' School, Didcot

The Ouija Board

I woke up, I saw blood on the walls and heard a loud noise. I went to my parents' bedroom and found a Ouija board on the bed. The door shut on me.

I heard someone saying, 'We're possessed!'

I screamed, I saw the door opening. I saw blood dripping down the door. There was a person with a knife and white eyes. It was carrying dolls in its hands. As it blinked it had black eyes. It was a black-eyed child.

A few seconds later, I realised it wasn't real, just a nightmare.

Abby Grace Santer (13)
Didcot Girls' School, Didcot

Haunted School

I have just arrived at the dark, empty school that no one goes to anymore, because one night a teenage girl was murdered there. But she never left, the body had, but not her spirit.

I walk past the school and I see a glowing light through the windows, just moving on its own. I know it's the poor, innocent girl, Sarah. She is all on her own, and has no one but herself in a dark, empty and gloomy school.

Aislínn McGuigan (13)

Didcot Girls' School, Didcot

Silence In The Library

Her eyes snapped open, the library was in darkness. Floorboards creaked and shadows flickered. She moved onwards. An eerie shriek flew through the air, but on she went, nails digging into her palms. Another noise and another, without knowing if they were real or not, she ran.

Fear, fear engulfed her. She could not, would not fight it. They were here for her, the spirits. They tore her heart, shattered her soul like glass. He mind was pierced and shards of shadows shot across her. Finally, she broke, she fell. A scream rang clearly through the cold, dark night.

Silence...

Vikky McRitchie (12)

Didcot Girls' School, Didcot

Chloe With... ?

Chloe was home alone at midnight, whilst her parents were out. As she was watching telly, there was a knock on the door. She didn't answer. She carried on watching TV, but it suddenly stopped working. It was all flashy, like lightning, scaring Chloe. It was dead silent, then there was a *bang* on the door like thunder. Chloe was so confused, she went under the table. But looking out of the window she saw scared faces outside. The men smashed the kitchen windows, came in with their bones popping out. They shivered, turning around with missing bones...
'Argh!'

Iqra Haleem
Didcot Girls' School, Didcot

Haunted House

Daisy was skipping down the street. She loved playing with her teddy bear. She saw a spooky house and decided to walk in. It had spiderwebs all over it, window to window, door to door. It was dark and gloomy. A ghost jumped out, he was very old and crinkly, so he thought he would scare her. But she automatically changed, with a click, into a demon tarantula! The ghost was frightened instead. He swooped off as fast as he could. She chased him with her hairy legs, then lived in the spider's webs happily ever after.
Creep, creep!

Chloe Louise Jacobsen (12)
Didcot Girls' School, Didcot

The Girl With Two Shadows

A shadow appeared, my shadow, then another – I now had two.
Whispers encircled as I walked through the deserted theatre. They
were surrounding me, screams were everywhere. Then a laugh.
As the light beamed down, they appeared once again. Following me,
following my every step, my every move, my every breath. I heard the
leaves on the floor being swept up by the icy breeze. I turned around,
they were never leaving me alone. I couldn't get away – trapped!
I saw a dusty, smashed mirror on the floor. Staring at myself, I started
to fade into my own shadow.
'Help!'

Daisy Duckham (13)
Didcot Girls' School, Didcot

Jeremy And A Vampire

Jeremy and Mike strolled into the creepy mansion, it was good to get
away from being a detective. Jeremy was scared, he hung onto Mike
like a bat.
After 30 minutes, Mike heard a scream. Jeremy was in a room,
because Mike and he spilt up. Jeremy saw a vampire.
'Hello,' said the vampire, 'I'm hungry,' he continued.
The vampire bit into Jeremy's neck, blood pouring out as the vampire
did it. There was a scream and then - silence.
'Jeremy?' Mike yelled, scared...

Davina Tyrrell (12)
Didcot Girls' School, Didcot

The End

We were innocent children, idiotic children. It was meant to be fun. It wasn't meant to happen like this. All my friends were dead. Every day another died in a new, gruesome way. We were haunted by something. Something bad.

I have never seen it, it kills in a flash, leaving only dead bodies behind. You cannot kill it, believe me, I tried. I am next. The next to die. It is coming. Moving through the walls to get to me. I would run, but where? There are no doors or windows. You're dead once you arrive.

I'm dead...

Megan Potthast (12)
Didcot Girls' School, Didcot

Untitled

I, Chloe, am standing in my empty school. I had to stay late to give my homework in. A shiver down my spine, the door opened but there was no one there. I ran as fast as I could, but oh, I ran into Will. Cute or what?

He saved me and took me back to his house. We had hot chocolate and sat by the fire.

Chlöe Jennifer Chadwick (13)
Didcot Girls' School, Didcot

Their Demise

The black mamba hisses menacingly. Sabina's eyes widen as she stumbles backward. It suddenly sprays venom into her eyes, corroding them into nothingness. When the convulsing corpse finally thuds onto the musty floor, hundreds of leering wolves leap from the shadows of the dark, crumbling mansion, tearing the flesh apart.

Adrian heard the nightmarish sounds, even through the thick oak door. He runs to a window and smashes through it, landing on his feet. Shadows rise up and jump across the walls.

'Sabina?'

Abruptly, an invisible force grabs his throat, choking him and starts to drag him to the underground…

Fatima Tuz-Zohra (15)

Emperia College, Luton

The Encounter

It was becoming night and I still hadn't seen the Yeti. I was thinking of giving up when I saw footprints in the snow. They looked like they were made by a gigantic ape, so I started following them.

After some time, I got to a cave, I looked in and it was pitch-black. 'Hello?' I called.

There was no answer. I snatched my flashlight out of my bag and ventured into the cave. I could hear the wind howling outside. I saw bones littered everywhere. I heard a sound behind me. Sharp claws glinted above me…

Umayr Zamir (12)

Emperia College, Luton

Midnight Chase

I sat silently on the bench, crying softly and staring up at the clear moon. I shivered from the cold. I could hear my own breathing, my heartbeat. The wind whistled through the leaves and over the lake. Then I heard footsteps. My heartbeat grew faster as I tried to hide. Something stopped behind me.

Scared, I started to run as fast as I could. I heard the footsteps give chase. Who could it be? I suddenly tripped, falling to the floor. I felt the creature's cold hand turn me around.

Going deathly pale, I whispered to the ghost, 'Dad?'

Sumayyah Baksh (13)
Emperia College, Luton

Solitude

A girl, who was abandoned at the age of five, lived alone in a dark house with broken windows. She loved to explore, but one fateful day, she bumped her head on something crumbling.

What was it?

She looked in front and saw a gravestone. She stumbled backwards. A bloody hand hovered around the soil. She held her breath, a cold shiver ran down her back. She ran home, crying in fear as she discovered scratches on her arm. Where did she get them?

That night, as she climbed into bed, she could feel somebody's presence watching over her shoulder...

Saira Khan (11)
Emperia College, Luton

Sins Of The Father

I'm running. I don't know why. I'm always alone, why am I not alone tonight? She is here with her brothers, Hel, Fenrir and the snake. Why now? Where are they?

Cautiously, I stop running and Hel comes. Fenrir kicks me to my knees. The snake is on my throat, choking me like the noose most people think I deserve (I really don't).

Ropes are snakes, I've decided. Am I dead? Not sure. No, this is not my fault! Oh, my name's Loki by the way. Three of my kids want to kill me.

Let there be light...

Eve Mundy (13)
Gosford Hill School, Kidlington

Friday Detention

Strolling out of form, I knew I had another long, boring Friday detention. This room was new. This classroom was mysterious. It had no windows or teacher in it. The edge of the classroom was filled with dolls. Why was this classroom filled with old dolls?

Carefully, I sat down in the dusty chair. Suddenly, one of the dolls, which was as old as the Victorians, started to move its head slowly. Suddenly, the radiator started to breathe out refreshing, cold air.

All of a sudden, the door shut, it was now locked. I felt something on my shoulder...

Ben Hague (13)
Gosford Hill School, Kidlington

The Attic

A new day, a new house. A shiver ran down my spine and I knew something was wrong. My parents were not at home, I didn't know where they were. I stood still and listened to the silence.

Suddenly I heard growling and violent smashing sounds from the attic. The closer I got, the louder it became. Trembling, I opened the attic door. It was pitch-black. The growling was deafening and the shadows of two deformed humans emerged from the darkness. One was holding an axe.

'Mum, Dad, is that you?' I cried.

Nadia Ella Rose Lowndes (13)
Gosford Hill School, Kidlington

The Nightmare

Searching, a librarian found an old newspaper with the front cover of three strange sightings of a mass murderer in California. *Crash! Thud! Thud!* She turned around and saw a shadow coming towards her. She screamed and ran out of the library and looked up. She was running down the road towards home.

She said, 'Why me?'

Frantically, she opened her front door and ran upstairs and locked her bedroom door. After thirty seconds, the front door suddenly smashed. *Smash! It must be the murderer!*

There were footsteps up the stairs and a big, bad baseball bat – it ended tragically.

Aaron Holley (13)
Gosford Hill School, Kidlington

The Wood Chase

Running through the forest, I spot an abandoned house with boarded-up windows. I look back, they're getting closer to me within seconds. I pick up the pace and head towards the old, battered door ahead. Why are they chasing me? Why isn't the door opening? Frantically, I bang on the door so I can be let in. The noises are getting louder and closer. The door swings open and I clamber inside. A man as tall as the house comes in. He looks me in the eye and I say to myself, *is this the end?*

Ben Martin (13)
Gosford Hill School, Kidlington

Nowhere To Run

Running down the spiral staircase, not knowing where to go, they run into a dark, stuffy room and can't see. A small light appears, they think it is finally over. They sprint towards it, praying there is a way out, their little hearts beating faster and faster until – darkness. 'Are we going to die?' Cautiously, they turn around, looking desperately in every direction, trying to see if anything is there. Suddenly there is a loud bang! Like a bomb went off. The place shudders. It is freezing cold. There's footsteps, getting louder and louder. Then they hear, 'You will die!'

Jack Launchbury (13)
Gosford Hill School, Kidlington

Too Late

Unwillingly, I found myself stumbling into the decayed church next to the lake.

I stuttered, 'Hello?'

I shot in, slamming the door behind me, crouching behind a pew.
A voice whispered, 'You should not be here.'

What was out this late? At church? Nervously, I dashed across the aisle, wishing not to be seen. But it was too late. A tall figure rose from the front row. Like a cheetah, it approached me. I felt a cold chill down my spine from the once-holy angel. I shut my eyes, hoping it was all a dream.

It was too late now...

Benjamin Male (13)
Gosford Hill School, Kidlington

Voices

Listening to music was the only thing that could calm me down. I turned my music off and I heard weird sounds. *Bang!*
'Ha ha.'

I stayed in my seat, I heard it again. *Bang!*
'Ha ha.'

I decided to go and see what all that was about. I thought to myself, *what's that? Where is that coming from?*

As I was walking up the stairs, I heard giggling. Then I could feel someone or something pulling me. I was being pulled to the attic. I went up, I was screaming, all I thought was, *where am I going?*

Ellie Eldridge (13)
Gosford Hill School, Kidlington

The Asylum

Creeping, I slowly make my way through the blood-infested corridors. Parts of human body lie scattered all over the place. Less than six months ago, this place was a working, lively mental asylum, but now the patients have disappeared. Where have they gone? That's what I'm here to find out.

Six months since the bomb was dropped here. I've heard of the inhumane ways it can affect people and when it was tested on animals, it mutated them into something the world had never seen. I trod cautiously. *Crash, thud!* I froze, I felt a hand grab me...

Cameron Fox (13)
Gosford Hill School, Kidlington

The Face

Screaming for their lives! The room was dark and all you could hear was the screaming, but who was it coming from? Was there any way out of this? Nervously, I opened the door to find a figure staring me in the face, like I'd done something wrong. It started to run towards me like a dog to its owner.

I finally saw who it was, they weren't human. A lion's head was fixed on the side of an old lady's head. The ears sewn together, half the face flapped, the face was half-human and the other half was lion.

Emily Brandish (16)
Gosford Hill School, Kidlington

The Beast

We were creeping along the path, the storm crashing around us. I felt frightened. We saw an old ivy-ridden castle, so we decided to take shelter. As the door opened, bats flew rapidly outside. We froze in silence. Should we really be here?

Frantically, we looked for a place to hide. Suddenly, I realised I was alone; my friends had disappeared. From the distance I heard a blood-curdling scream and the evil cackle of a monstrous beast. I ran down a gloomy corridor, I was lost. I could hear the beast getting closer. I hid.

Suddenly the door swung open...

Jacob Orton (13)
Gosford Hill School, Kidlington

The Short Cut

'That party was amazing!' shouted Phil.

Ellie stretched out and pointed to a road.

'Should we go through this way? We'll get home quicker,' she asked. Phil agreed. The moon was shining, giving light to be able to walk. As they walked through the short cut, they reached an abandoned graveyard. Out of nowhere a high-pitched voice whispered, 'Run!' They quickly ran across the graveyard and entered the abandoned church. Silence. They stared into each other's scared eyes.

Bang!

Lili Vieira (13)
Gosford Hill School, Kidlington

Awful Weather

Walking into the church, the sound of thunder makes me realise I shouldn't be here at this time, this day and with this weather. But I have no choice. The flash of lightning lights up the stained-glass windows around me as I go for the top. I grab the rope like nobody's business, but then I realise it is somebody's business, as I hear the chilling words, 'Your time has come.'
I feel a hand down my back and hear blood dripping. I realise my time is up, it's over...

Joe Otter (14)
Gosford Hill School, Kidlington

The Walk Home

The walk home from Ben's was always boring. This night sky had a white glow from the moonlight which made it easier to see than normal. I'm guessing someone like you wouldn't be bothered to walk all this way in the dark.
Nervously, I started to speed up my walking pace, which wasn't normal, because usually I'm not scared of anything, but the man with no eyes took me by surprise. His eyes were like lumps of charcoal. They spiralled like a blackened tornado.
Within seconds, my eyes were now his own eyes, forever.

Mason Smith
Gosford Hill School, Kidlington

Mysterious Awakening

It was a misty, dark night and I could see figures moving around the house... it was a gloomy, dusky night and I could hear people awakening... it was a miserable, horrifying night in the forest and I could hear people shouting... I could feel shadows following me around, like a spider crawling up my spine. From the corner of my eye, I could see the ghostly spirit.

It wanted me to go with it. Then I found out it wasn't a ghost at all. I had gotten lost and led myself here. To this abandoned, overgrown and frightful house.

Maddie Kemp (13)

Heybridge Alternative Provision School, Heybridge

Skelly Claws Comes To Town

You'd better not shout, you'd better not cry, you'd better run or you will die... Skelly Claws is coming to town. He watches when you're sleeping, it's worse when you're awake, he kills you with a chainsaw so run...

She was sleeping and a loud smash came from downstairs. She woke to find a thin figure outside her door.

'Mum?'

She was wrong, he entered her room. His bony fingers grabbed her from her bed, holding her tightly by her neck. Her lifeless body hung in his hands. She dropped to the floor.

Watch out! You might be next...

Tara Edwards (12)

Highdown School & Sixth Form Centre, Reading

The Killer

I woke at 2am in the morning. I couldn't sleep because I had a nightmare. It was about burned people. It was scary.
After I woke up, I saw that my window was open. I closed it and tried to sleep. I couldn't. I felt that someone was watching me. I turned around, I saw him. The door was open and he told me, 'Go to sleep!' Then he jumped on my bed, trying to shoot me in the head using a silenced pistol. He did it. My mum found me dead on the floor.
Written from Heaven...

Mikolaj Kajetan Misiewicz (13)
Highdown School & Sixth Form Centre, Reading

Don't Do It!

A month ago he died in a car crash. His girlfriend was devastated. She couldn't take it, it was getting to her. She began to self-harm, locking herself in her bedroom, crying for hours.
It was Christmas which we were spending in New York. Not a good idea. We went to the Empire State Building, which was an even worse idea. We were looking at the building.
'Where has she gone?'
She was at the top of the building. We tried to talk sense into her, it wasn't working. We started to panic – she wouldn't jump, would she?

Katie Hill (13)
Highdown School & Sixth Form Centre, Reading

The Abandoned Cabin

One night, a group of friends all joined together for Halloween to go trick or treating.

After going to a few houses, they got lost. It looked dark and misty, they couldn't see anything. *Bang!*

'It is a door,' one of them said.

They looked around and they saw trees, no houses except this one... it was abandoned, so they opened the door. Clowns, clowns everywhere. Clowns with smashed faces, blue Afros and then one of them turned round and said hello.

All of them turned, they ran.

They screamed, 'Help!'

The clown got up from its shelf and jumped...

Deyana Harmony McKiernan (13)

Highdown School & Sixth Form Centre, Reading

Can You Guess It?

Its small head peeks out from the little hole in the wall. Eight legs help it move around and create a home. Many are scared of these horrible things even though this creature is smaller than them. Terrorising everything, big or small, they come in different shapes and sizes.

Have you got any idea what it could be?

They take over corner by corner with their thin webs. They watch you all the time. Sometimes they are all over your home! Hairy bodies and small fangs. Ready to kill their prey.

Still not guessed it? It's a spider!

Ellie Drake (13)

Highdown School & Sixth Form Centre, Reading

Vanished

It was on Christmas Day when I was haunted by my friend. He was possessed by an evil spirit who wanted to take over my body so he could live again.

I was in my kitchen chopping up food and I heard a bang, so I ran to the sitting room and searched my house. When I came back to the kitchen the knife had gone.

Later that evening, I went into the kitchen to turn the lights off. As I did I heard a bang in the kitchen, it was the knife, stabbed into the chopping board.

Niamh Herbert (12)

Highdown School & Sixth Form Centre, Reading

The Edwardian Doll

It was Christmas Day, Amy was the only one at home, but didn't realise something was watching her. She looked under the Christmas tree to see if anything was there for her. There was a big present. She brought it into the light where she unwrapped it. It was a doll with long brown hair with a blue Edwardian dress covering her body.

It was getting late, so she went to bed. The doll rose from the box and made her way upstairs. She went into the girl's bedroom, she sat on her bed and slit the girl's throat.

Naomi Tappern (12)

Highdown School & Sixth Form Centre, Reading

The Never-Ending Flame On Christmas

It was Christmas Eve when the world fell silent. My house was left, the corridors never stopped, the doors were voids to a black hole. I followed the corridor, it was my only choice; it never ended. More darkness after every step. Until a wet drop hit my face! I felt it with my finger, it was blood! The world was in hell.

Finally, I saw light, it was a flame. I tried going near it, but it grew every step I took. I threw water over it, but the water just evaporated. I turned and saw a large wall!

Harvey Wright (12)
Highdown School & Sixth Form Centre, Reading

Once Played, Many Killed

'Come home, but don't leave', this is what the letter reads. *'Open and watch, but don't leave'*.

She put the DVD in.

Midnight on the third day. *'Lock the doors, he'll still find you!'* Mysterious symbols flickered on the screen. The first day, she was a non-believer, the second day she studied the symbols. The third day came, looking constantly at the clock. It ticked slowly. The fear rushed. Something was watching and watching closely.

The time came, she locked the doors and windows. *Tick-tock, tick-tock* in her head. Three... two... one... the clock struck twelve. Dead!

Alex Tonkin (12)
Highdown School & Sixth Form Centre, Reading

The Haunted House!

One mysterious day, in a spooky town in the middle of nowhere, a family moved into a home that was once a haunted pub. They had no idea of this.

When the girl walked into her massive room, there were no windows, which was horrible. She didn't expect this. Sally ran downstairs to tell her parents, but they were suddenly gone. She ran back upstairs and all she could see was loads of cobwebs everywhere. Sally looked everywhere and still could not find her parents in this horrible, creepy, scary, dusty haunted house.

What was she going to do now?

Alyshba Sassoon (12)
Highdown School & Sixth Form Centre, Reading

The Apocalypse

I woke up hearing screams, gunshots and sirens. Slowly I got on my shoes and stepped outside. Zombies, blood and death was all I saw and smelt. Quickly, without making a sound, I stepped into my car.

I accidentally ran over a walker and drove off to find a safe place to go. I saw people banging on my car window, but I kept driving.

I arrived at a shopping mall hoping that people were here. All of a sudden, a walker jumped on top of me, trying to tear me up, bit by bit.

A shotgun sounded...

Libby Louise Gutteridge (13)
Highdown School & Sixth Form Centre, Reading

The True Colours Of Santa

I'm dead. Well, I thought I was. I'm making this clip to warn you about grave danger; Father Christmas, Santa, he's... he's evil. He was the one that ended my life.

It, um, it started when I heard a noise.

'You'd better not cry, you'd better not scream, you'd better not run, it's Santa!'

The stairs creaked, you can guess where it went from there.

'You'd better not squirm, I'm telling you why, Santa Claus is coming to your room!'

The door abruptly blew open, but no one was there. The lights switched off. *Click!*

'Argh!' That was me, Arthur.

Rory Edwards (12)
Highdown School & Sixth Form Centre, Reading

Clown Town

It was pitch-black when I got here to Clown Town. I was unaware of this place, all I knew was that it was full of orange-haired clowns who chased you around the town. It was the scariest experience of my life. Clowns are my biggest fear. I had to go there to get food for my family. The aim of the game was to go around the village and find food without getting caught. Unfortunately, I was unsuccessful in escaping. I'm still here now, we've been here for hundreds of years. It is still pitch-black.

Vickey Kios (12)
Highdown School & Sixth Form Centre, Reading

The Unborn Child

In a normal family of three, with a normal dad, mum and a girl, was a bone-chilling tale of the unborn child.

'Daddy, why isn't big brother in the family photo?' were the first words Lucy said.

'We don't have another child, you're the only one.'

Days, months, years had passed and Lucy started talking to herself. Dad was concerned about her, so he asked her, 'Who are you talking to?'

'Big brother, his name is John.'

Shivers ran down Dad's spine.

'How do you know that?'

'I told her,' whispered an unknown dark figure.

Dad turned...

Binson Gurung (12)

Highdown School & Sixth Form Centre, Reading

Manic Times

It has been over six months since my sister died. Me and Melody were in our room, when suddenly a man climbed in through the window and strangled her. I ran and hid under my bed. He stopped and ran off. I slowly crawled out and saw my sister lying there on her bed. From that point, every night, I hear screams and choking sounds. Sometimes I wake up and see it all happening again. All the time I wonder, if he will return.

Then, one night, it all happened again, but this time he went for me...

Charlie Fuller (12)

Highdown School & Sixth Form Centre, Reading

The Dark

Pitch-black; I couldn't see a thing. Curled up in my bed, hoping
not to get a visit. Almost asleep, I started hearing footsteps. I could
hear creaking of the floorboards. It was getting closer and closer. It
stopped. It was about one in the morning. I picked up the phone and
rang my friend. I was talking to her for about two hours.
I hung up and tried to go back to sleep, but I felt breathing on my
neck. I looked up and saw a black mist in the corner of my room. I
froze. What a night.

Zeynah Hussain (12)
Highdown School & Sixth Form Centre, Reading

Happiness Never Lasts At Christmas

It all started on Christmas morning... the stockings were full, everyone
was asleep in bed... the atmosphere was full, waiting with joy.
Later on in the day, we were all eating the turkey that was delicious.
We were full of laughter and happiness. I have always said happiness
never lasts in life – and so it didn't...
Most of Christmas I spent focused, sat in hospital near my sister,
she was only six. She was such an intelligent girl. She had been
wandering around the Christmas tree, playing with the lights and
decorations. We all miss her...

Grace Douglas (12)
Highdown School & Sixth Form Centre, Reading

Frostbite

A winter wind whistled in Ben's ears, his black funeral tie dancing on the cold breeze. He was icily satisfied: Uncle Moe was dead. That part-time prisoner stole and sold many an item – what's more, his attitude stank of bitter anger and his clothes of tobacco. Ben's boots tapped the brick street as head-shaped fog rolled into chilly oxygen. Rimy arms of air played with his scarf and jaws of frost bit his face. A figure of murk wandered towards him. Ben felt more biting. Mist floated into a skull shape, and bit Ben again. It was Moe's skull.

Joe Jones (14)
John O'Gaunt Community Technology College, Hungerford

Silence

It was late when I finally accepted I was lost. The fog was creeping in, the forest was rapidly darkening. I sighed and reached for my omnipresent phone, but I couldn't find it, so I chose a random direction and started walking briskly.
It was cold for autumn and where there should've been soggy leaves, frost glittered beneath stark branches. I spotted some crocuses crouched by a shrub. Odd. If it was spring, there should've been birdsong, but it was silent under the trees. Completely. I couldn't hear my heartbeat, I realised as I fell to the ground. Where was... ?

Hannah Glover (13)
John O'Gaunt Community Technology College, Hungerford

The Old, Young And Deadly

The gnawing sound inflicting the echoing hallway sounded like the arthritis of the building's residents. I stepped in, then pressed the button, sticky with a treacly ectoplasm; a buzzing voice, gasping, said the floor number. The surrounding mirrors speckled with wrinkles and freckles again, like its residents. Bold rose water and cat pee wafted around the elevator. Doors opened. Silence. *Creep, creep, creep,* across the wine-red carpet, I knocked on the door.
The door opened... No one. The darkness was like a cannibal, swallowing me whole. It digested my sinewy body against the crumbling, old wallpaper.

Rachel Cooper (13)
John O'Gaunt Community Technology College, Hungerford

The House

There was a flash! My eyes blinked, where was I? Was I at home? No, I was in a room. What room? I stood up, legs shaking. There was a noise coming from outside. The corridor! Footsteps came closer and closer and stopped at my door. The door handle creaked. I ran to the window, it was locked! What was I to do?
The wardrobe! I stumbled to the wardrobe, opening it I jumped in. Coats of some sort were hung up. I stepped back.
'Argh!'
I turned around onto my stomach, an axe came down. *Splat!* I felt nothing.

Phoebe Piper (13)
John O'Gaunt Community Technology College, Hungerford

I Didn't Choose The Slug Life

'Here it comes!' I screamed as the ghastly creature approached me. Its huge, bear-like hand pulled out a crystal-clear object, filled with great white balls. It was salt! The salt fell onto my tough, slimy skin and started to burn holes through my delicate flesh. I could feel and hear the sizzling of my insides. My heart was thudding in my eardrums.

Why did the creature pick me? I am just an innocent slug. After what seemed like forever, I thought it must be the end. Then something weird happened, I woke up, it was a dream.

Molly Lewis (13)
John O'Gaunt Community Technology College, Hungerford

Boom, It's A Bunny

It is coming, it's chasing after me, I can hear its footsteps. It is close. Nobody else is around. Just me and this creature. I can hear my heart pounding against the walls of my chest. It's making a sound, it's trying to communicate with me. It's near.

The tunnel seems to last forever and ever. The footsteps are becoming closer. As I carry on running, my heart beats louder. My breaths are heavier. My footsteps wider. This is life or death. I can't carry on, I turn, behind me is a very cute bunny.

Georgia Smith (13)
John O'Gaunt Community Technology College, Hungerford

My Change Of Life

'It is coming, everyone, come quickly or it will get you! Follow me at once.'

The creature began to charge towards me, teeth white, eyes red as blood.

'Argh, please don't hurt me,'

It stopped at arm's length and looked deep into my eyes. I was lifted, my vision of the world had changed. A mighty howl the creature gave, fire swarmed around me. Its ear-piercing howl had descended and the fire transformed me into... into... I can't explain, it's too much to bear. Eyes red, white teeth, grey fur.

I was none other than a ferret!

Morgan Henderson

John O'Gaunt Community Technology College, Hungerford

Inside Your Head

It is Halloween and the sun can no longer be seen. It's the time when vampires and dollies come out to play, but where will they stay? Under your bed or how about inside your head? Killing you in your sleep or gobbling up all your dearest memories. Will you be next? If your door creaks, you know they're here to make you disappear. There's no hiding, no one to protect you, just you and your fear. Will they choose you? Most probably, just be ready to expect them, anywhere... !

Molly Munro (14)

John O'Gaunt Community Technology College, Hungerford

Forest Murderer

I was taking a nice, slow walk through the old forest next to my house. I hear something, a loud crack comes from behind me. I ignore it, thinking it is just a twig. I carry on walking. I hear another crack, this time I turn around. I see nothing.
I carry on walking till I hear my phone ring, I answer it, only to hear some loud breathing. I start to get really creeped out, so I speed up to get home quickly.
Then suddenly, I hear a loud thud and that is the last thing I remember. Black...

Rebecca May Shailes (13)

John O'Gaunt Community Technology College, Hungerford

Boo, I Found You At Last!

I was running, something was chasing me! I stopped, it had disappeared. I was panting like a dog, worried about who it was. Then *bang!* I screamed, I fell to the dark, damp, dreadful floor. I heard a massive, ear-piercing sound; it was the floor cracking. I fell with a massive thud!
There was a pile of old, dry, cracked bones from dead people. I started to panic, what was happening to me? Why was it happening to me? Then someone touched me with a cold, bony, skinny hand. I was stuck, never to be found again.

Jordan Joanna Susan Mosdell (14)

John O'Gaunt Community Technology College, Hungerford

The Terrorist

One stormy night, a spine-shivering, skinny-to-the-bone wolf stood and let out a huge howl. While this was happening, something else was going on. There was a man against the world, a terrorist, just lurking about in England with a bag filled with weapons, explosives, hand guns and assault rifles, you name it.

He stood in an alleyway, watching everyone walk by. Suddenly, he decided to pull out a gun. He shot everyone walking past, then did a runner.

The police checked who'd died to see what could have killed those very innocent victims.

Leon Davies (11)
John O'Gaunt Community Technology College, Hungerford

Coins

I stared at the grave. I remember placing the coins on her eyes. Were they there long enough? What if she's still there, living? I shuddered, the light was drifting away like fingernails clawing at someone's face. Fog was curling its hand round every grave in a tight handshake. Suddenly, a scream. It was light but piercing, a sword stabbing evilly, aiming for my heart. I turned... a face, mud in mouth, tossing, turning. Another scream.

'Help!'

Who was this? Then I noticed the coins, reality struck me. A scream, I know who this was. It hit my heart hard.

Evie Chester (11)
John O'Gaunt Community Technology College, Hungerford

Untitled

Late night walks were the best, through the graveyard with the lads. I heard a crack, like a shotgun. It turned out this walk wasn't so good after all. I ran and found myself entering an old, derelict church. I knew I'd be okay.

Sitting by myself, on an ancient, run-down pew, I desperately tried to ring Matt. But he wasn't picking up. I then saw a sinister shadow coming towards me, creeping along the walls, expanding the dark and doom towards me.

'Someone help me!' I cried silently. 'Someone help me, please!' I screamed. 'This is not good.'

Beth Pollard (14)
John O'Gaunt Community Technology College, Hungerford

In The Warehouse

Working my late-night shift in the warehouse, I suddenly heard a noise. I shot around briskly, no one else was there but me! A gloomy figure was sat smirking at me. The forklift turned on. All of a sudden, I heard the screeching of tyres. Before I knew it, I was rapidly running through the warehouse, dodging sharp utensils, knives and daggers flying.

My heart felt like it was coming out of my chest, it was beating so fast. The screeching and revving of tyres and engines stopped.

I woke up from my nightmare.

Ella Moyle (14)
John O'Gaunt Community Technology College, Hungerford

Silver

Whilst examining the deceased body of a local lawyer, an adventurous mortician called Virginia Clifford, manages to unearth a folk tale about a supernaturally cursed, silver firearm circulating throughout New York.

As soon as anyone uses the revolver, they have approximately one hundred and sixty-eight days left to live. How was Virginia going to unravel the dilemma?

The only clue was that once the gun is photographed, there is a withered ghost holding the revolver. Was the murder an accident or was it a brutal, horrific massacre? Only the ancient, filthy revolver and ghosts know. Will Virginia know soon?

Edward Peter Hawkins (13)
John O'Gaunt Community Technology College, Hungerford

The Unstoppable Beast

Lightning crashing through the sky, thunder pounding like the Devil's drums. As lightning split the air, a formidable creature arose from the ever-dark swamp on the outskirts of town. As the night darkened, the creature spread its wings and took off as fire spat from its mouth. The townspeople had heard of this incredible beast, but they never thought it was real. People ran in fear as soon as they saw the creature flying above the houses, burning anything that got in its way. Everyone needed to stop the incredible beast, everyone tried, but it was unstoppable...

Thomas Morgan-Matthews (12)
John O'Gaunt Community Technology College, Hungerford

The Town That Changed In A Day

Abandoned, that's what it was, the town had been around for centuries, but that day it was no longer around. It was full of terror and danger. Children were screaming with fear, whilst their parents anxiously tried to find them. *Bang!* Another bomb fell. A group of men came and dumped the bodies on the cart.

As I slowly walked out of the alleyway, a burst of flames threw me back to the wall, with force. My heart was racing, where was I and was I alive? The last thing I remembered seeing was a lonely child running towards me...

Ellie Bampton

John O'Gaunt Community Technology College, Hungerford

The Spine-Chilling Shape

As I was walking through the inanimate snow-cloaked forest, I saw a dark shape. It would have been clear what or who it was, if it hadn't been at night.

The shape came closer and closer! I could now see that it was a hooded figure. The figure came so close I could smell its foul breath. It looked up to howl at the full moon. As it did this, its hood fell back to reveal something worse than its breath. Lengthy, bloodstained teeth hung over its flabby bottom lip. A substantial amount of fur obscured its keen eyes...

Molly Rixon (12)

John O'Gaunt Community Technology College, Hungerford

The Risen Dead

Walking slowly through the thick, gloomy fog, I saw a dark, abandoned house in the distance. I got closer and closer with every step into the unknown.

When I eventually got to it, I walked in and my spine shivered. It was dark and I was terrified. A bat came down from above, I jumped out of my skin. When I walked into each room, I had nerves flowing through my body.

When I went into the third room, a dead body lay in front of me. It rose up and I ran until I lost it, gasping for breath.

Aaron Lord (11)
John O'Gaunt Community Technology College, Hungerford

Trapped

The moors were silent, eerie, terrifying. I was running, trying to think. A shapeless blanket of fog came down. There was something there, I'm sure of it. I screamed but the fog acted like a buffer, separating me from the outside world. The black shape which had frightened me so, was still in pursuit. I daren't look back.

My house was very close now, I stumbled on a stone and staggered to my feet. Reaching home, I fumbled the door open. Once inside, I started to make a cup of tea, but I noticed the fog, creeping under the door...

Katherine Natton-Bell (11)
John O'Gaunt Community Technology College, Hungerford

Boo!

I awoke in an abandoned house, alone and afraid. I moved back as slowly and sluggishly as I could. I took a deep breath.
I whispered, 'Is anybody there?'
Creak! came a noise. A cold hand touched my warm back.
'Who are you? What do you want?' it said.
Bang! came a noise, *bang,* it came again, but louder.
'Shh, they are coming, hide!'
The walls closed in, the light only illuminating the centre.
'Stop!' I cried. 'Leave me alone.'
'They are coming.'
'Who is coming?'
'Shh, they are here, hide quickly!'
Suddenly, there came another bang.
'Boo!'
I awoke.

Chloe O'Brien (12)
John O'Gaunt Community Technology College, Hungerford

Afraid

Walking in the forest, I could hear the birds whistling and the sun was flickering through the trees. It started to get dark and I could see shadowy figures in front of me. I turned away and ran! I could hear footsteps following me. I didn't know what to do. I kept on running, I was out of breath. I could see them, I could see them as clear as day; their black, shadowy figures.

Their breath smelled like a bin that had not been emptied for a year. Their eyes were black and piercing. Their faces, wrinkly and old.

Kerry Louise Hillier (11)
John O'Gaunt Community Technology College, Hungerford

The End Of The World

I start to run... my ankles crimson from cuts and scrapes. I glance back, screams and shouts, scarlet stains on the ground, they don't stand a chance... I check my gun, three bullets left. I must use them wisely. I don't have a clue how I have survived this long.

The sky's a horrible mix of colours, steel grey and jet-black. The monsters start to advance on me, their gaping mouths filled with black teeth. *Boom! Boom!* Two down, I have one shot left, out of the blue jumps another, I shoot and miss – my vision blurs...

Theo Carreck (11)
John O'Gaunt Community Technology College, Hungerford

Untitled

One dark and gloomy day, Bob was having a brisk walk when he saw a dusky, gloomy, abandoned house. When he had a thorough look, there was a figure with something in its hand. The figure vanished as quickly as it came. It reappeared behind Bob. He just carried on walking to the old, terrifying and abandoned house. He went closer, he heard a petrifying noise.
As he got closer he realised what the noise was, it was a group of teenagers having a scary, but bizarre conversation. Bob fell to the ground, sweat trickled down his face.

Christopher Hillier (11)
John O'Gaunt Community Technology College, Hungerford

The Apocalypse

Sweat flooded my forehead, my body was barricaded from my thoughts. I had a signal from my mind, so I took the shot. Silver bolts swam through the air, piercing the victims, causing their heads to explode. Four more 'things' appeared, one crawling, the other three on their feet. The crawler clawed at my leg, tearing my skin, pulling my flesh. The pain spread through me like a virus, inducing me to collapse.
I pulled the trigger of my weapon four times, hitting all four of the zombies. Then my vision slowly died...

Sam Featherstone (12)
John O'Gaunt Community Technology College, Hungerford

The Silent, Snowy Day

One wintery, snowy day, a flush of seagulls fluttered over my large house.

'Woof, woof,' my dog, Roxy howled.

'Be quiet for the thousandth time,' I fiercely replied.

I grabbed the lead and attached it to my loud, active dog.

On the way to the shop, a lot of events happened. First of all, over the zebra crossing, a boy racer zoomed past me within about six inches of my body.

'Roxy, Roxy, no... ' I shouted in despair.

Bang! I started to feel tears in my eyes. Was Roxy... ? Oh, was it her or a different, alive object?

Bradley Elliott Smith (11)

John O'Gaunt Community Technology College, Hungerford

That Night

One night, I woke to the sound of lightning strikes. There were groans as I heard a sudden *crash!* My blood ran like a river's current. I screamed, then I jumped under my covers. I could only hope they would disguise me from them.

The scorching, sticky habitat surrounded me. I felt the hot sweat dribble down my face. I wanted to jump out and face it, but my body left me and did not. My body began to dry out, I felt like time was beginning to be wasted. Was I going? I left my body forever.

Zoe Maidment (11)

John O'Gaunt Community Technology College, Hungerford

Darkness

On a dark winter's night, an old man had deep wrinkles like ravines and a dark black hat that was filled with rain water as clouds deposited their waste on the streets. The man was walking home from buying goods from a local shop. Suddenly, mystical problems occurred, like cars driving themselves to the moon, turning black. Everything was like a game, where players took over and caused mayhem.

The man saw and reacted to the problems by running. He dropped all his shopping as he tripped over a falling tree branch. He never made it home.

Max Hunt (11)
John O'Gaunt Community Technology College, Hungerford

Untitled

One dark and gloomy night, when Vincent fell on a stumpy rock, he got up and he saw a mansion. Then he saw indescribable things. Then, when he tried to run away, he knew he was going mad. He thought the trees were blocking the way.

After giving up trying to get away, it started to get foggy and Vincent went inside the mansion. He knocked on the door and it creaked open, then a tall, dark-figured man jumped down the old, tatty stairs with a thud. Vincent was stuck there, until a painful, horrible death.

Ellis Buju Morgan (12)
John O'Gaunt Community Technology College, Hungerford

The House

Creeping through the seemingly never-ending corridor, he clapped eyes on a door with the most diminutive crack. His mind ready to be imploded. He peered through the door and saw... nothing! Before he could touch it, the door slowly became ajar... and before a drip of his sweat touched the ground the door came off its hinges and the soul-stealing scream of a ghoul penetrated his soul!

As his body fell to the ground, her ghost was set free and he was to take her place for all eternity, until another oblivious peasant was to be lifeless.

Corbin Swabey (12)

John O'Gaunt Community Technology College, Hungerford

The Rumour

It was a murky, gloomy night. The rancid smell of rotten flesh filled the air. The abandoned, run-down house was plastered with blood smeared everywhere. The wind flew through the shattered window, whistling as it went. It was as bitter as ice. The huge house stood in the middle of a dark, deserted forest, riddled with bloodthirsty wolves, detecting the smell of fear in an instant.

There was a rumour that a decrepit, lonely old man used to live in the house. It was believed that he'd killed his wife by pushing her off the roof in a vicious storm.

Daisy Lockhart

John O'Gaunt Community Technology College, Hungerford

The Man With The Twisted Eye

'So, tell me what happened Sir.'
'I should start from the beginning...
The sun was peeking over the hills and already the Chanders were reconsidering letting this madman into their home. They and their son were halfway across the sodden field. Police sirens blared as they parked on the muddy track outside the field. The Chanders got safely to the police and the madman was arrested for attempted murder.'
'Who was he?'
'The man with the twisted eye?'
'Yes, but his name, who was he?'
'Well my friend, he was the son of course!'
'How?'
'He's me... !'

Ceara Lynne Fowkes (12)
John O'Gaunt Community Technology College, Hungerford

The Uninhabited House

On a dark, dingy night, the deluge of rain covered the young boy who adventured into the old, uninhabited house at the bottom of the road. Hurriedly, he entered the house, but within seconds, a putrid smell hit him. The smell was so bad, he vomited in disgust. He ran to try to escape, but the door slammed shut and locked.
He went up to the bedroom, but as he entered the room, there, in front of his eyes, was a decayed body with flies eating the flesh.
The young boy heard a shriek and was never seen again.

Cory Hale (14)
John O'Gaunt Community Technology College, Hungerford

The Never-Ending Candle!

The candle that was lit, was upon the old, rusty fireplace. It was a cold, windy house and the candle flickered as the old man walked into the room. The man blew the candle out and went into his modern-made bedroom.

Then the candle was suddenly set alight again. The candle had moved ever so slightly and the light was shaking. It was as if a ghost was trying to blow it out. The lights suddenly blew out and there was a light inside the candle. The spark of light was lit again. The candle was unstoppable.

Molly-Jayne Moore (14)

John O'Gaunt Community Technology College, Hungerford

Christmas Eve

Christmas Eve, normally a fun time, however, tonight was different. Instead of being cheerful, it was dark and gloomy. I lay in bed, shaking with fear. I had seen something through the crack in my wardrobe. What was it? A glistening eye? Then I heard a deep rumble of sound.

'Ho, ho, ho!'

I wanted to scream, but if I did, I knew I was dead. Instead, I threw my covers over my head and hid, scared to lift my head. I fell silent, I heard breathing coming closer and closer...

Then, *bam*, I was never seen again...

Ellie Griffiths (13)

John O'Gaunt Community Technology College, Hungerford

Deathly Shadow

The blood-gurgling demon lurked in the darkness of the night, searching for a vulnerable, bewildered victim and chose one perfectly. Tom was depressed as usual. He knew it wasn't easy to walk the dark, gloomy streets of London. He had been thinking about how he was left at his date.

According to the restaurant cleaner, she had climbed out of the... he stopped, he felt a growing, searing pain in his abdomen. Tom screamed out, but there was nothing to be heard. He fell to the ground with pain, as his sight went out, as the shadow crept closer...

Oren Fowkes

John O'Gaunt Community Technology College, Hungerford

Deserted Town

A lone stranger wandered along, down the damp, murky street. Bottles were clattering across the floor. He looked up at a dark cloud lurking over the distraught town. The stranger began to wonder what was around the next dangerous twist and turn.

He suddenly realised that he wasn't alone. He dashed through an alleyway, screeched to a halt and stopped. There was a bomb planted there. The timer said ten minutes and that's how long it would take him. He shot off like a rocket, shooting through the passage. Eventually, seeing light, he dashed and ash poured over him.

William McLaughlin (11)

John O'Gaunt Community Technology College, Hungerford

The Mythical Creature

It smelled earthy as I strolled through the damp, dark forest. *Crack!* I turned – nothing. Confused, I started to walk faster, trying to find my way home. Another crack. I spun round to – nothing. Then a growl. I froze. Coming out of the shadows, beady red eyes pierced my own. I was paralysed. The creature growled, it echoed through the forest. My eyes widened as the animal, which I could now identify as a wolf, maybe a werewolf, lunged at me and shoved me to the muddy earth. It growled once more, pain was the last thing I could feel.

Chloe Langford (14)
John O'Gaunt Community Technology College, Hungerford

Deserted Church

I crept into the church, which was deserted. The door shut raucously and the suspense came when the composition started playing deafeningly. It was blood-curdling. Lightning made it feel sinister. I unobtrusively stalked down the slippery stairs into the basement. The decayed body fell from the roof, making me jump.
I went closer, it leapt out at me, making my hair rise like a lion about to slaughter its prey. I scurried away like a cheetah to the exit. It wouldn't open, I was going to die. I felt the shiver and sensed the blood – dying – vanished...

Ciaran Morrison (13)
John O'Gaunt Community Technology College, Hungerford

Untitled

It was a dark, stormy night. I was alone in my house, I was really scared because I heard a voice. It was a deep female voice. That voice called out, 'Help me please.'
I was really scared. I said, 'How can I help you?'
The scared voice said, 'I don't know, but help me please.'
Then I saw her, she was ghostly. The bright red blood dripped down her face slowly. It was creepy and scary and I felt really cold, but I don't know why.
A door closed with a bang...

Alex Vasko (14)
John O'Gaunt Community Technology College, Hungerford

The Dark Night

It was dark, he was walking down the murderous road on which his brother's life was taken; slowly visualising his sibling's sinister death right before his eyes. He felt the distress from that night. The shock from the moment the car was whipped from the road. He smelt the petrol slowly leaking out of the car next to the burning engine bay.
Bang! He heard the explosion in which his brother died.
Shaken, he awoke from his terrifying dream. Quickly he looked beside him and there was his brother, dead, in a body bag.
'I killed him!'

Liam Benson (14)
John O'Gaunt Community Technology College, Hungerford

The Cottage

James and Meg were strolling through the woods one night and heard the crack of a stick.

'Hello?' shouted James.

There was no reply. They kept walking. After what felt like an hour, James and Meg saw a foreboding cottage with blacked-out windows. The cottage was old and abandoned. It had a sign on the front door.

'The sign is written in a different language,' said Meg.

'French or German?' asked James.

Meg nodded her head.

'Let's go,' said James as he opened the door into the cottage.

As the door opened shivers went down their spines...

George Maslin (13)
John O'Gaunt Community Technology College, Hungerford

The Beautiful, Ugly Twist

Once upon a twisted time there was a beautiful, popular girl who everyone fell for. Her imagination was going wild, like a rough, desolate wind on the rugged moor. Scars travelled all over her arms and bruises up her legs.

Everything was suddenly changing; her white teeth were sharp like daggers, her arms as lanky as long trees. Pale white face with dark, piercing eyes that stared like old pictures in a deserted castle. When this happened, everyone referred to her as the unpleasant, ugly, deserted girl. Everyone would stay away as she now lived unhappily ever after.

Chelsea Smith (14)
John O'Gaunt Community Technology College, Hungerford

The Graveyard

Fog crept between the graves. A boy briskly ran through the graveyard, hurdling over the graves. The sinister boy tripped over the corner of a grave, he got up and turned around. There was a skeleton, holding a long, sharp sword. The boy cowered into the corner of the graveyard.

The skeleton reached for his dagger in his pocket and pelted it at the boy like a rocket. It pierced straight through his hand. He slumped onto his hand, holding one in the air, the skeleton approached and sliced the boy's head off like a knife through butter.

Matthew Lugg (14)

John O'Gaunt Community Technology College, Hungerford

Untitled

My eyes were dry, my nose was frozen as the wind hit my face whilst I was running desperately to get to civilisation. I knew something was watching me, but I didn't know who or what.

My heart raced as I got to the church gate, my fingers were numb, I could barely move them. It was stopping me from shutting the gate. I had no choice but to run on before I would get caught.

Cautiously, I walked through the church, my head was almost throbbing with all the thoughts I had. A deathly hand brushed my face...

Georgie Prismall (11)

John O'Gaunt Community Technology College, Hungerford

The Mystery Of Jack Blackburn

I clutched it, my hands dampened the newspaper with sweat. It said:
'Unknown how Jack Blackburn has mysteriously died tonight at 11pm'.
I stormed outside, angry, slammed the paper down and walked down
the musky street.

Someone came up to me, said hello and asked what my name was. I
told them I couldn't say and I walked away.

Then someone else came up to me, saying the same thing. I said the
same thing back. They walked away. This may seem strange but it's
because my name's Jack Blackburn.

Isabelle Barnes (11)
John O'Gaunt Community Technology College, Hungerford

The Butcher

Legends speak of a man who had one task in life; reap the remains of
battle. His hulking mass shook the ground, his putrefied, rotting flesh
decayed all round him. He was The Butcher.

Since wars with corpse-ridden fields are no more, he replaced
another ancient nightmare. The clattering chains of his meat hook
and the dull thunk of his cleaver, infamous. He sought out Old
Krampus and devoured him. Smacking his chops and licking his
cleaver, he picked up Krampus' sack and went off to continue his job.
Where will he go next? Have you been naughty or nice?

Jordan Luke Bartlett (17)
Kennet School, Thatcham

A Serial's Game

Thick fog surrounding the abandoned cemetery. Another dead body was being placed in the grave. Another murder.

The following night, there was a howl and a scream coming from inside one of the family tombs. Another murder.

The police and criminal investigators searched the perimeter, and nothing. Suddenly, another screech came from the far side of the cemetery, it was the lead inspector this time, his throat was slit, his heart on the lifeless ground.

Everybody started to panic and their torches went out. One by one, every officer was killed in a different way to represent their personality.

Emily Walker (17)
Kennet School, Thatcham

The Warning

Ominous wind encircled the ground beneath her feet as she gazed upon the depths of the lake. This was the exact spot Amy vanished from just a week before. The moon stared at the red scarf draped on the hedge; was this the warning?

She inspected with the dark pits of her eyes to piece together any evidence to help her before the gusts of the blasting winds stole it from her.

Every twig snapped simultaneously to her breaking bones. Her lifeless body was swiped away as the voice screeched a low and chilling laugh...

Bethany-Jo O'Neill (17)
Kennet School, Thatcham

Knock, Knock, Who's There?

I don't know why I'm here, they dared me to break into this rickety, abandoned school. It's pitch-black and my flashlight is starting to flicker. I won't stay here long, I'll just leave now. Mum will be getting worried. I'll call her. No signal and the door seems jammed. I didn't lock it, I haven't got the key.

Empty chemical flasks, paper and broken desks surround the place, you can almost hear the canes whipping bare flesh. Wait! What was that? A door creaked open, it's probably just the old caretaker. But what kind of caretaker holds an axe... ?

Emily Thomas (16)

Kennet School, Thatcham

Shot In The Dark

Blackness of the night, darkness descends upon the living, fearing the shadows as they creep upon your soul and spirit.

'Hello!' the voice trembles and quivers like a glass about to smash. 'It's me!' she screams into the vast hole of humanity that greets her. Her hair, her nails, her looks, her voice. All nothing when there's no one around. A lone wet whisper greets her eardrum.

'No one can hear you scream!'

Why her? What did she do to deserve such a fate? Was it him? Was it him who put the noose around his own neck?

James Elstone (16)

Kennet School, Thatcham

The Mill

James and Connor set out in the darkness of night one foggy winter evening. They had heard noises the night before, down at the old, abandoned mill at the end of the cow field by the river.

Climbing the barbed wire at the end of the field, they edged closer still.

Standing with the mill towering over them, they heard a scream and a thud.

Connor tried the door, put his shoulder against it and budged it open, only to see a meat cleaver driven deep into a man's skull. He turned to run, only to see James' body - dismembered.

Aran Willett (16)

Kennet School, Thatcham

Horror House

Run. Running, darkness crowds in. Blood trickles down my arm, I gasp for breath. I won't make it, I'm their celebratory feast. The moon blinks through the gnarled trees, the wind whispering silent secrets about the trespasser. I stumble upon the ghostly Victorian house standing in isolation.
'Where's Cathy?'
She was behind me.
'Cathy?'
I open the gate, it rattles with fright.
'Cath?'
The anxiousness growing slowly. *Smash!* I run into the house, the monstrous pool of blood leading upstairs where my older sister should've been. I run upstairs, then I feel it, the cold, bony hand on my neck...

Kareena Kaur Tooray
Loxford School of Science & Technology, Ilford

The Haunted School

Two friends, Emily and Jessie, went to the same school. It was
Monday, they were going back to school after the holidays.
They arrived at school, but there wasn't anyone there! They both
remembered that school didn't start until Wednesday. They were
about to go home, but the door was locked.
Suddenly, all the lights turned off.
'We've been set up!' exclaimed Emily.
There were loud banging and hissing noises coming from the gym.
The noises kept coming closer and closer each second. They heard
the voice of a man.
'You will never get out!'
Could they ever escape?

Faiza Waheed (13)
Madni Institute, Slough

The Alleyway...

As I was walking down the alleyway, the darkness surrounded me,
branches swayed, making rustling noises. The wind blew fiercely,
pushing me along. My stomach rumbled with hunger, my skin pale
like the moon. Weakness overcame me, my head started spinning,
causing me to fall. I tried grabbing on the rails beside me for support.
Suddenly, without warning, something hit me from behind. There I lay,
not knowing whether I was dead or alive.
I awoke to the sound of heavy footsteps. As my eyes began to open,
they grew big upon seeing a shadow ready to attack me...

Hajira Jamil (13)
Madni Institute, Slough

Sinking Feeling

On a boring Monday our exam results came in. The whole class got less than 80%. Suddenly, the Professor came in with a concoction, he spilt it all over us and we shrank. Then everybody panicked. How would we become big again?

We searched for an answer, then found a map leading to a place where one wish is granted - but the journey was full of obstacles and danger because we were tiny.

We set off. Insects were like monsters, people were like giants. It was dark when we found the wishing well, but now we were facing hairy lizards!

Zainab Ahmed (11)
Madni Institute, Slough

The One In Etiolated Silk

My blue heels scrape across the wooden, mucky floorboards. As I inhale the poisonous air, I sense frustration. All the exhilaration for an immaculate holiday in Spain, gone to waste.

As the sinister gentleman with a shabby coat leads me to my room, I gaze at the white robe floating across the room. Its black, intense hair gliding through, with her cadaverous hands beside her raw-boned waist. As she glides across the room, I start to remember the myth, except it's no fable. The formidable scars on her feet... could tell she was the one never ever to summon...

Raiha Noor (14)
Madni Institute, Slough

All Hope Was Lost

Tears ran down my cheeks, my sobs faintly echoing through the pitch-black blanket of loneliness. I was chained, alone, arms outstretched to the wall, feet strained so tightly that I could feel the rubbery material piercing mercilessly. I could hear clattering ringing in my mind, my eyes would shoot open. Every, what felt like an hour, my soul managed to escape, my head thumped out of fatigue. Every bit of energy I had was an attempt at getting unbound.
That particular moment, I realised I would never be found; my heart dropped to my stomach. All hope lost.

Maria Jabeen
Madni Institute, Slough

Lawfully Detained

When I came to, I was strapped to a chair with a single light above me. Light shone to every inch of the sterile room. As I struggled against my restraints, a door opened, in came an unsmiling woman in scrubs.
'You're finally awake. We were worried the phase one surgery had caused permanent damage to your brain.'
'Surgery? Phase one?' I croaked.
'Oh yes. At True-Mind, we endeavour to uncover the best in you, contrary to popular belief.'
At the term 'True-Mind', I knew I was at a reprogramming centre: a facility for the mentally unstable.
'Begin... Phase Two!'

Sumayya Aisha Ali (14)
Madni Institute, Slough

Abandoned

Painting the sky, the blood-red sunset entered the cracks in the windows, highlighting silhouettes of where empty souls once laid.
'You hear that?' I said, while questioning the approaching echoes.
Silence.
'Cindy?'
'I hear it,' she said stumbling over her words.
'We need to get out now!' I exclaimed as I devised a plan.
'Agreed,' she whispered, focusing her eyes on the surroundings.
With her shaky, icy hand a nod of reassurance and the twist of an unknown doorknob... chaotic, beady-eyed bats bombarded the air space. Now screams replaced the silence around the once lonely, helpless house.

Sara Muhammad
Madni Institute, Slough

The Graveyard

I ran a bit slower, as there were holes pierced through the ground. Suddenly, I heard a blood-curdling scream. A cold chill ran down my spine. I stumbled to the ground and saw a skeleton lurking on the edge of a bin. Where on Earth was I? How did I get here? Darkness crowded around me, I could feel a magnetic force pulling me to the ground. I ran as fast as my legs allowed me. All of sudden, an icy hand clutched my shoulder, then I realised I was in a graveyard...

Manzil Khan (11)
Madni Institute, Slough

Possession

A mysterious breeze came from behind the graveyard door. I saw many graves surrounding me with floating spirits screaming and haunting me.
'Help!'
No reply. The rusty door handle of the church was covered in dust and cobwebs. I looked around and noticed a possessed young boy lying on the ground. I ran until I could stop hearing tortured voices. I fell and I knew the boy was getting closer. All I heard was footsteps. The boy got closer, I got up. I ran as fast as my feet could take me. It was too late, the boy caught me…

Aisha Khan (14)
Madni Institute, Slough

The Moment

The bathroom door slowly creaked as I hid behind the dark curtains. I had nowhere to go, but I knew one thing, I wasn't alone. A sharp scream pierced the air and my heart started thudding louder and louder, closer and closer. I could feel she was behind me. I had summoned her, thinking it was a game.
I blacked out. I opened my eyes to see Paradise on my right, Hell on my left and a balance in front of me. This was the moment where my future would be decided.
Hell or Heaven? I couldn't be saved…

Laura Daghes (14)
Madni Institute, Slough

Flee From The Sinister House

We all crowded around the board game. Abruptly, the lights died. Dad went to go and check it, it was a fuse. My elder brother insisted on going to the toilet, so my dad let him, finally!

After sometime we heard a ferocious howl from the toilet. In distress, we all ran towards it and the lights came on.

On the floor we saw my brother's body, lying in a pool of blood. On the mirror, I saw the words: *Who's next?*

In fear, with a lamp, I smashed the mirror into smithereens and we escaped from the sinister house.

Laiba Qadeer (14)

Madni Institute, Slough

You're The Victim

You trip ahead of a dark, ragged figure. It has a black hood and a thick black cloak that trails behind. Hot red fire cries out from its eyes, nostrils and mouth. It has a skull for a face that's so pale it emits a pearly glow. The wind rustles against the cloak seams, revealing the rest of the dirty, cracked skeleton. It reaches out its hand, with fingers as sharp as blades, and drags them along your face.

No sound escapes your scream. It scrapes down the rest of your body and you're slowly drowning in your own blood...

Maryam Rahman (12)

Madni Institute, Slough

The Spooky Alleyway

As dusk fell, I was still walking down the old and creepy alleyway, searching for my mother. As I went deeper and deeper into the alleyway, the fog was getting mistier. I heard a spooky sound, which sent a shiver down my spine and dark shadows surrounded me. I didn't know what to do, other than just keep going forward. It felt as though I was in a terrible nightmare.

I urged myself to wake up, but I was still walking down the lonely alleyway. Suddenly, something grabbed my hand and pulled me away harshly, my screams sharp and piercing...

Afiyah Ahmed (13)

Madni Institute, Slough

One Escape

Death... my life is terrible, that's not even a good enough word to describe how much I hated it.

All of a sudden, a burst of lightning broke the sky apart. I was really frightened, my heart was palpitating. I ran so fast to see what happened; many thoughts entered my mind. The sky and ground were in complete darkness. I was clouded in thought.

Suddenly, I heard a familiar sound. *That's not good!* It was a car! *Bang!* I fell to the ground, blood came rushing out, there was no escape, no way out, just death!

Sumaiyah Naz Naz Bhatti (13)

Madni Institute, Slough

Descending Midst

The air whistled, and through every blade of grass crawled a multitudinous silence; caressing the unseen, flowing through the unknown; comforting the absent.

The lady hadn't yet stirred from her unassertive slump, instead sat motionless on the bench. The world's a bygone, lost in the midst of life. The sun drifted along the clouds, a lost nomad, not a beacon of warmth and light.

She was there still. I'd expected she'd have moved. The ground shook again. I thought, *he's hungry now*. I felt lost, but really, we all are. In the midst of life we are in death.

Stefan Darling (14)
Reading School, Reading

It

I was in. My heart was racing and blood was dripping from my veins – *drip, drip*. Casual steps from 'It' were bugging me. They ran through my head over and over. I thought these sounds were the last things I would hear. Struggling to breathe, I belted the words out – 'Help! I need help!'

Or at least I thought I did. My beseeching voice was quiet. I knew this was the end.

'It' came again, 'It' was angry this time. In fact, 'It' seemed to be screaming now. Suddenly, I felt a ray of hope reach me.

'It' was dead!

Sanskriti Sahoo (12)
St Bartholomew's School, Newbury

Mummy And Daddy Left Me Alone

One day, my wife and I were downstairs watching TV, my wife had a bad history of seeing apparitions in our house, but it didn't bother me.

Around six o'clock, we heard a girl's voice coming from upstairs.

'Hello!' Giggle.

We shrugged it off, but over time we grew suspicious, so we went into the hall to look.

There we heard a voice again.

'You have made a bad decision.'

Then we sprinted for the car and drove away. We returned to the house in the morning and found, written on the wall: 'Mummy and Daddy left me alone'...

Alex Rance (12)

St Bartholomew's School, Newbury

Death On The Tower

Death – the soul-crushing word that destroys every glimpse of hope. The word clings to my mind. The word that controls my every move. My arms, smothered in blood, my chest flared in pain. I couldn't move; I was paralysed, thinking how fast death would come.

Loud footsteps echoed up the tower and there was the hideous face that was going to murder me. He strode forward and grabbed me with his invisible strength. I screamed. I cried. The pain bolted through my body like lightning through a tree. He smashed the window.

I managed one feeble word, 'Help.'

Frankie Lochhead (13)

St Bartholomew's School, Newbury

Dark

'There are things you don't want to know about the dark, Son. Weird things have been happening at night. Around here, people have vanished, street lights have fallen over without cause. Things grow by day... so that they can conceal things at night. Unknown things. Nobody knows why. People watch over you by day... but at night, they go. No one can protect you. People die at night, Son. Be careful, when the fog comes in is when the unfortunate events start. People get injured.'
I slowly looked down at where his legs should be. They were just stumps.

Harry Clarkson (12)
St Bartholomew's School, Newbury

Sweet Nightmares

The moonlight glowed in my dark, shadowy eyes. Forest trees loomed precariously over me. Then screams filled my ears. Closer, closer still. I started running for my life. I suddenly stopped and fell to the ground. My beloved ones, be there for my sister, for I no longer can, it seems. My eyes became bloodshot and I looked to the starry sky. Death loomed over me, blocking out the moonlight glow.
'Who are you?'
I felt my heart disappear from my body. Where did it go? Death encased me with the thought of it getting me – alive. Sister, Gomenasai Aishiteru...

Ellie Starling (13)
St Bartholomew's School, Newbury

There's Someone Under The Bed...

Dad came to tuck me in tonight. Strangely, my room felt safer with Dad. Outside is gloomy and stormy and I can sense that something bad is going to happen. I know I sound like a big baby having Dad come and tuck me in, being 12 and all. But he's all I've got left. As Dad kisses my forehead, I feel something stir under the bed. Suddenly, the light goes out; there's a thump on the floor and I instantly realise it's Dad. I look at the floor which is covered in blood. My brother is back...

Anna Kelpi (12)
St Benedict's Catholic College, Colchester

Salvation

Fires forever ablaze, men howled, perishing in eternal anguish. Their mouths formed shapes to make words, but the sizzling pile of tongues told me all I needed to know. Dark angels beset the pit and howled out an unholy laughter while they feasted on the tongues. Above them stood a creature, a monster beyond description. Its pure wickedness filled the pit and as he growled the dark creatures bowed in complete submission.
But wait – there was a new scream. A man, bound in chains was being thrown into the pit. He screamed and this time I heard him clearly.
'Salvation!'

Treasure Chimsom Chima (13)
St Benedict's Catholic College, Colchester

Beware Of Crimson Peak

The wind howled as Rose and Mary walked through the gates of Crimson Peak. This was the house that was thought to have been abandoned for hundreds of years. Tonight was the night when they explored it; to see if that was the real truth.

The girls walked through the entrance, making the smallest of sounds. That was until Rose let out a piercing scream which caused Mary to whip round. She didn't see Rose, but a tall, slim man appeared from the shadows. He spoke in a very sly tone. 'You shouldn't be here, it is not safe!'

Frances Broatch (14)
St Benedict's Catholic College, Colchester

Night, Night Mummy

It was a dark, stormy night. A night one would want to forget. It was cold and the boy was shivering, longingly, he stared at the rotting corpse; his mother. Tears fell from his eyes as he brushed away the wet mud to reveal the face that he once looked up to with love. The rosy cheeks and happiness she once had were now gone. All his precious memories of her, now tarnished by this horrifying event. Pulling the knife out of the body, he was reminded of when he went to sleep.

Eyes closed, he said, 'Night, night Mummy.'

John Lynch (15)
St Benedict's Catholic College, Colchester

The Burning Fire

The sun did not rise for the light did not shine. The dreary night was approaching, for death was nigh. The fog drowned me in the depths of despair. Alone, trapped with no sense of life, the crackling of the fire continued to burn. The cry for help and the sound of regret, did not overcome the unchangeable fate that awaited me.

As the fire approached, I prepared for death. No sign of escape, just an image of a burnt body invaded my mind.

The flames licked at my feet, my vision became unclear and I knew no more...

Daryl Cother (15)
St Benedict's Catholic College, Colchester

The Job

A normal day. That's what I told myself when I got into my car. Clumsily trying to find the ignition with my battered key, I noticed them. Finally firing the engine, I pulled out of the shadowy car park fast.

I drove, the streetlights adding a piercing orange to my ambient, blue dials.

Suddenly though, I saw them again, a growing speck in my mirror. I floored the accelerator, hoping to get away, only to be met with a red light. I stopped. They stopped alongside. Both their tinted windows came down...

Dmitriy Koshonko (15)
St Benedict's Catholic College, Colchester

The Long Walk Home

The bus doors hissed and I was left on the pavement, alone. I'd be home soon, the only thing that was between me and safety was the alley. Mist hazed my view of the end. I shivered, my own shadow startling me. The street light flickered. The gate at the end slammed shut; someone was behind me.

'Hello, is anyone there?'

No answer. I carried on walking. I heard footsteps, I walked faster. The gate was stuck, the footsteps were getting closer. The gate jolted open, I felt a sigh of relief as I shut the door. I was safe.

Phoebe Dyball (14)

St Benedict's Catholic College, Colchester

The Scream

I woke up to piercing screams. I quickly ran downstairs to investigate what had happened. Terror and alarm overcame my body, my instinct was to run into the arms of my dead brother. Blood was everywhere and I felt as if I was going to drown in it.

Swiftly, I ran outside, screaming for help, but it was no use. Alone and exposed, I found myself standing in the middle of a ruptured neighbourhood. The wind howled like a wolf and threw a cold breeze into my arms. My shout echoed, I realised this was my first mistake of many.

Luigi Sombilon (15)

St Benedict's Catholic College, Colchester

Christmas Fright

It was Christmas Eve. All was quiet; not a sound to be heard apart from the crunch of footsteps on fresh snow. First I heard the screech of the rusted gate opening, then the footsteps drawing closer. Suddenly, the lights on the Christmas tree started to flash violently. As the footstep drew closer, my heart beat faster.

I crept quickly down the stairs, I could sense something wasn't right. The footsteps stopped, a shadow loomed over the door, blocking the outside light. A hand came through the letterbox, reaching to the handle. It unlocked the door, opening it.

'Santa... ?'

Niamh O'Neill (13)
St Benedict's Catholic College, Colchester

Under The Bed

It was a Halloween night, I was sitting in bed and suddenly I felt something poke me in the back. Then I thought to myself, *don't panic, it's just a popped spring.* But then it happened again and again, so this time I chose to look under the bed. The worst thing a kid should do!

Then the worst thing happened – there was a... *clown* under the bed and from that moment on, it got worse and worse. First there was two, then three and then something was scratching the door. The door opened and I was gone... !

Milly Thurston (12)
St Benedict's Catholic College, Colchester

The End Of Time

Mist was everywhere. There was a flash of light, I woke up and at the end of my bed was a red Mexican tarantula. It was the biggest man-eating spider alive!

It was about to attack, when suddenly, out of nowhere, came an army of mini-spiders. They attacked one by one. This was the end of me. *Dun, dun, dun... !*

Daniel Claxton (13)
St Benedict's Catholic College, Colchester

Egyptian Nightmare

Into the pyramid I went, so scared. The door shut behind me and dark corridors were waiting for me to pass through. I slowly walked through and at the end was a young girl, singing *Ring-a-ring o' roses*. She tripped me up and I fell down a dark hole filled with creepy-crawlies and bugs. I sprinted and a skeleton started to chase me. I fell and I ran into a door. On the door was a code I had to figure out. I ran to ditch and a load of bats caught me!

Jessica Brown (12)
St Benedict's Catholic College, Colchester

The Ghost Caroller

The fog was rushing in from the field, covering the churchyard. I walked towards the church behind the cemetery. The gate to the graveyard was rusty and I could not open it, so I used my climbing skills to climb over. I hopped down and the fog rose up and covered the whole of my body.

Cries and laughter started to surround me. I was frightened, then a Christmas carol started to get louder and louder! I ran to the church, slammed the door and hid under a pew, shivering. The noise stopped and there was a cold breeze...

Dawid Kurzawa

St Benedict's Catholic College, Colchester

The Haunted Tunnel

I went into the tunnel and when I went inside, I heard little children singing, 'Ring-a-ring o' roses'.

Suddenly, I felt a cold shadow on me. Then I heard the noise of water dripping. I was running to get to safety and I felt like someone was behind me. So I kept running and looking back.

I fell over a stone; that was the end of my story of the haunted tunnel...

Yanira Allen-Meha (13)

St Benedict's Catholic College, Colchester

The Big Snake

I was on a mountain with my friends. We did a trip and I did Scouts, so I was with my Scouting friends.

We were walking and someone screamed, there were ten snakes! We started to run, but the snakes were too fast. I was running really fast and then I stopped, there was a little snake that had two tails. One really little and the other really big. I was scared.

I ran back, no one was there but more snakes.

Five minutes later, I became a snake too...

Beatrice Nardi (12)
St Benedict's Catholic College, Colchester

The Creepy-Crawlie Spider

I was in my bedroom and I saw a big spider. It had large legs. I asked my dad, 'Can you get it out of my room and take it outside?'

Then there was another spider, the same one had come in again and it went up onto the ceiling. My dad had to get a ladder this time and get it down from the ceiling. Then my dad was walking with it to the window, but he dropped it. My dog came up and ate it, every little bit. My mum hadn't come in because she was scared!

Ellie-Mae Pledger (13)
St Benedict's Catholic College, Colchester

Untitled

A fierce wind blew the damp cardboard, gaffer taped over the window. *Bang!* The door swung open and slammed against the drab wall. In the door frame stood a large, broad-shouldered figure. Its steps shuddered the floor and, what appeared to be mace, made a spark as it dragged along the concrete that it had previously stood on. A long, loud, low-pitched sound came from the figure. A flash of lightning came near the window and the light shone across the figure. The figure approached me, it came closer, closer, right up to me...

Raymond Ese (14)
St Benedict's Catholic College, Colchester

The Chimney Ghost, The Creeper In The Chimney

I was walking through the gate and saw a big, massive building. It was in the fog, it was all black looking. Abandoned, the wind blew the fog over the building. I walked to the house, I opened the massive door. Curiously, I sat down, it was very dark.
Suddenly I heard something coming down the chimney.
'Who's there?'
There was no answer. Then a creepy figure came out of the fireplace. It was ten feet tall, it was the chimney ghost!
'Please don't hurt me.'
It scratched me across the chest with massive claws. I ran, I escaped!

Joseph Guild (12)
St Benedict's Catholic College, Colchester

The Possessed

Eeeeee! As the hinges creaked, the sound of gloomy, lifeless souls filled the room. I seemed to be alone, although, mentally crowded by possessed killing demons. The smell took me instantly back to a graveyard that was rotting intensively. I was standing on a pitch-black piece of brick that was crumbling rapidly by the second. Cradles, motionlessly waited to catch its next prey; knives waiting to penetrate through skin and axes ready to go on a date with the gullet.
This was the day, the 3rd of March, time: 12:30am, could I survive?

Sam Rundle (12)
St Benedict's Catholic College, Colchester

Tick... Tock

The big metal bell in the abandoned town struck. *Bang! Tick-tock...*
tick-tock... No one lived in this town, it was eerie, creepy, but yet so alive with the sound of footsteps along the savage path.
There's a story of a man who every night, goes up to the big metal bell and chants endlessly. *Tick-tock... tick-tock...* and he's never been seen. They say he's bleak, hollow and a broken soul, but that's not true....
'Wake up James, you'll be late for school!' said Mum trying to juggle the pile of clothes.
'Sorry, I was dreaming... '

Amber Coultrup (14)
St Benedict's Catholic College, Colchester

Savage Jungle

The constant buzz of the jungle was nauseating. I felt like a sane person growing mad with the jungle. The squawks of birds like vultures, hunting me down. Insects were eating me alive. Everything looked the same. I was caught in a maze of plants and towering trees that otherwise would be beautiful, but were now laughing at me as I struggled between them.

Sweat dripped from my throbbing forehead. I could hear every plant, beast and insect hissing at me violently.

'Help!'

My shout was lost in the savage jungle.

Rose Jones (13)
St Benedict's Catholic College, Colchester

Silence...

Silence. That was all I could hear. The loud kind of silence. I tried to move my hands, but movement wasn't an option. All that happened was the rusty clank of chains; the ones that were binding my body to the metal spear in the centre of the room.

As I looked around, I saw dust particles floating around in the beams of light. The hooded figure slowly drifting towards me. I could see the red of its eyes and the whiteness of its skin. I saw everything, but then I could see no more...

Zoe Pearson (13)
St Benedict's Catholic College, Colchester

He's Here

Leaves rustled in the distance. Each distinctive sound destroyed the eerie silence. I was too scared to blink. Never before had I felt so close to death. He was after me, I knew there was nowhere to hide. The wind picked up its pace, making my hair blow in front of my face. My heart started to pound in my chest. The rustling of the leaves seemed louder. He was here and he was coming in my direction. There was nowhere to run. Trees blocked my every move. I started to panic, he was almost there.

Someone breathed down my neck...

Marie Sofia Sebaratnam (14)
St Benedict's Catholic College, Colchester

The Voice

The door slammed, I froze, completely still. The wind chimes sang, the crows squawked. Then there was silence. As I slowly walked forward, the floorboards creaked and I squealed with fear.

The door swung open and a gust of wind blew in my face as I whipped my head around. I heard a voice, it sounded like it came from beside me. Suddenly, I heard it from somewhere else. Whoever it was, or whatever it was, was moving fast.

It dropped silent. I breathed a breath of relief. I felt a cold hand on my shoulder... this was it...

Emily Louise Pavey (13)
St Benedict's Catholic College, Colchester

Trapped

Dead or alive? His body stood motionless, frozen in time. His face disfigured and wounded with eyes holding an unreadable expression, his body screaming for an escape. Someone or something was responsible. Someone or something had inflicted such fear in the heart of what used to be a man. Trapped, alone, reduced merely to an attraction, a show, a form of entertainment and what for?
So men could laugh at his misfortune or gloat in the face of another human being. The demons of the past forever haunted me, reminding me of mistakes I'd made.
It... it was me!

Benita Mansi (14)
St Benedict's Catholic College, Colchester

Midnight Guest

Dong! The clock struck midnight. Amber could hear nothing except the faint snoring of her parents as she tossed and turned in her bed in excitement for her long-awaited birthday.
'Help!' screamed her brother.
She rushed to his side to find him drenched in blood, she then yelped for her parents, running to their room at the end of the hall, only to find two more corpses overpowered by blood trickling from their bodies, weaving in and out of the wooden floorboards.
She turned in fear to ring the police, greeted by an unwanted guest.
She screamed, 'No-oo!'

Delphine Masterson (13)
St Benedict's Catholic College, Colchester

Christmas Poison

Mother was a good woman, but sometimes she was bitter, very, very bitter.

Visitors were to be arriving soon.

It lay on a platter, so slick. Its radiance spread to each corner of the room. The first lady walked in, it was Mother's enemy. Why was she here?

I couldn't concentrate, all I saw was the pudding. Mother had said not to touch. It was meant for an enemy. But she could always make another one, so I did it. One bite led to another. I was so dizzy, so weak. So dead!

Now I understood everything she had said.

Elizabeth Igbinoba (13)
St Benedict's Catholic College, Colchester

Check Your Back

Days turned to weeks and I was still stuck in this desolate desert. No water, no food, just the sun as a blanket and the stars for love. I felt isolated.

I called, 'Hello?' But no one answered. A grumpy howl came from a strange creature. I followed the sound with eagerness.

Minutes turned to hours, my search for a living specimen was just a wish. Until – a small man howled again. I turned and looked at him, it felt like a hallucination. I pinched myself until my hand turned numb. I was still awake, until *bang,* I was shot!

Anthony Oluwapelumi Sanyaolu (13)
St Benedict's Catholic College, Colchester

The Refuge

Ben stared across the night, the thunder blew his eardrums to smithereens. He needed refuge; quickly. Then he spotted a garage, he ran across the open road through a derelict door. Spanners, screwdrivers and pliers lay everywhere on the dusty floor. The garage door squeaked shut – trapped. He grabbed the nearest tool and held it high.
'Come at me whoever you are, I'm not afraid,' he threatened.
The thought ran through his head; trapped. Then, to his right, a hammer moved. He thought he was hallucinating. An engine started to run, car lights lit up the ceiling. No escape – trapped... !

Bandi Cserep (12)
St Benedict's Catholic College, Colchester

The Waiting Game

Waiting, everybody does it. Like a child awaiting Christmas, I was awaiting his next move. A living chess game. I heard some footsteps, the rain hammered down like a million tonne bag of rice. I slowly backed further into the room, listening to the boiler coughing, fighting to stay alive; I, on the other hand, was locked in a store room waiting for my departure.
Then there was nothing. The rain had stopped, the boiler was dead. I was sitting in a pool of sweat but freezing cold. Then I froze solid, my chest hurt, I fell into nothingness.

Jamie Baker
St Benedict's Catholic College, Colchester

The Dark Below

Fog was floating low above the ground. The wind was howling, the forest's undergrowth engulfed my feet. I was slowly sinking like a helpless animal in quicksand. A dark figure was lurking around me. Waiting. The forest bed had now swallowed nearly all of me. I couldn't do anything about it. It had covered my mouth. I was waiting to see what was in the depths below.

Suddenly, the dark figure vanished. I looked around me, but couldn't see a soul. I didn't know what was happening. Finally, I was gone. All I could see was the dark below.

Cieran Montgomery
St Benedict's Catholic College, Colchester

Game Over

Nothing moved. Nothing dared to move. The darkness was reassuring, the light would bring death. I knew not why, but how. I knew not when, but where.

Footsteps echoed amongst the shadows. It wouldn't take long for him to find me, but it was a chance I had to take.

Creak! The branch snapped, giving away my position. I fell flat upon my face. The apparent situation was still unclear to me. Should I run? Could I run? I froze.

In the glistening moonlight, I saw his face, perfectly contoured. He spoke in a warm, menacing manner.

'It's game over!'

Julian Olivagi
St Benedict's Catholic College, Colchester

Circus Carnevil

My heart's in my throat as I gaze wide-eyed at the spinning acrobat, suspended by a thread in her teeth from the apex of the tent. Abruptly, a cacophonous roar tears through the silence as a band of repulsive creatures, disguised as clowns, burst into the ring, armed with gargantuan chainsaws.

Firstly I applaud, thinking it's part of the act, until they start their violent rampage. Terrified spectators run madly, desperate to escape, lives intact. Dozens decapitated, crushed, disembowelled. Diving under the tent wall, I run, breathlessly and blindly. Suddenly, a chainsaw revs and rears up in my face...

Maddie Barrell (12)
St Benedict's Catholic College, Colchester

The Day I Lost My Brother

We ran to the helicopter, through the crumbled remnants of Trafalgar Square with a whole horde behind us. It had been two years since the start of the zombie apocalypse, we were informed that there was a refugee camp in the USA and we were able to get a place there. The zombies were much faster than me and my brother and soon caught up with us. Just as I entered the helicopter, I heard a deafening scream behind me. I looked back and saw my brother being ripped to shreds. We then took off, I was safe... for now.

Tom Brown
St Benedict's Catholic College, Colchester

A Tail As Dark As Night

I'd done it. Mother said I shouldn't, but I'd done it. I'd gone into the forbidden forest. I don't know why, there was just something about it that drew me in deeper and deeper.

There I was, running from this thing. It was like a shadow, but once it came so close it touched me, it was all furry.

Next thing I knew, I was on the floor with a great pain in my head. Huge and dog-like, the shadow climbed onto my chest and waved his tail in my face. I'd become one of them.

Chenile Sulley

St Benedict's Catholic College, Colchester

Scream!

The rain smacked down on the roof and the lightning struck without warning, whilst James lay in his bed. When all of a sudden, there was a scream from inside the house. His heart was beating uncontrollably and his hands were unable to stop shaking, shivering and shaking in fear, he crept downstairs, afraid of what he might be up against. He checked every room but one. As he carefully opened the door, he found a little old woman hiding in the corner, his eyes focused, he immediately noticed she was pointing to something. He turned around slowly...

'Argh!'

Jay Alvarez (13)

St Benedict's Catholic College, Colchester

Barbaric Brother

Bang! I lay there, warm and welcomed. Then again, *bang!* There was someone here. I crept down, daring to make any noise. I went in and out of every room but one, my little brother's. Forcing myself to, I smacked the door open and saw nothing but a pair of blood-red eyes. Then my eyes followed down to the cold, silver knife in my brother's hand.

A shot of fear and numbness hit my spine and paralysed me with fear. As my barbaric brother laughed hysterically, he sank the knife into my body.

This was it... the end.

Anton Alvarez (13)
St Benedict's Catholic College, Colchester

Under

As the rain hammered down on the crumbling gravestones, I heard a haunting voice call my name. A thick, grey fog loomed in the distance, making my vision mottled and unclear. I whipped my head around the corner, a blood-curdling scream rang through the forest. The hairs on the back of my neck stood up; a cold shiver ran down my back.

My feet started to sink into the ground; I tried to resist. Skeletal hands yanked on my ankles, pulling me down far into the corpse-ridden ground. I tried to fend them off; it was too late...

Olivia Farry (12)
St Benedict's Catholic College, Colchester

Bang! Bang!

The woods were the perfect place for Hansel and Gretel to plan their revenge.

That night, they crept up to their house in ear-deafening silence. They hid behind the old oak tree. Hansel wickedly smiled to himself while Gretel kept her thin icy lips shut. With a gun in one hand, Hansel opened the door, edged in and headed straight upstairs to the master bedroom.

The creaking door swung open as they entered. *Flick.* Two lights shone brightly. Two dreadful screams were heard, followed by two gunshots. *Bang! Bang!*

The house was filled with a spine-chilling cackle.

Freya Richardson (12)
St Benedict's Catholic College, Colchester

'Mummy, I Want That One!'

It is always the same. The girls gasping and pointing at my gorgeous blonde curls and lacy pink dress. Parents gasp at my bright blue eyes and blood-red lips, so they take me home and put me on the bed; completely unsuspecting of what I am capable of.

The police will show up a few days later, reporting a gruesome murder. Parents hang from the ceiling, children with knives through their hearts. They know it is murder, but they will never catch the killer. They put me back on sale, until a girl cries, 'Mummy, I want that one!'

Shannon Payne
St Benedict's Catholic College, Colchester

Untitled

One horrible and misty night, I was walking through a wooded cemetery from school. There was an old, abandoned church covered in vines. The door was half open, the padlock on the floor. I slowly opened the door.
'Grrrr!'
It was terrible, all the benches were broken, the stained-glass window was almost smashed to pieces.
Then I heard a noise...

Joseph Edmans (12)
St Birinus School, Didcot

A Night On Cemetery Street

On the 31st October 2015, everyone woke up to a bright red sky. From that moment on, they knew this Halloween was going to be different.
Suddenly, the ground was covered in a thick, misty fog. When night fell, there was an eerie atmosphere in Cemetery Street. I could hear zombies groaning, witches cackling and wolves howling. The hairs on the back of my neck stood up. I looked out of my window and saw every kind of monster you could imagine.
Then I heard the sound of gravel crunching under someone's feet, there was a knock at the door...

Sam Will (12)
St Birinus School, Didcot

In The Cemetery

One day, Bob decided to go to the cemetery at night to see his grandad's grave. He saw it and went towards it and then shone his torch at it. He was very freaked out because his torch started flickering even though he'd put new batteries in it.

Just before he came out, he heard the trees rustle and then the bush. He saw the ghost of his grandad, so he dug up the grave, no body. His grandad came up to him and pushed him into the grave and that was Bob's last scream that anyone heard.

Jack Greenaway (11)

St Birinus School, Didcot

Trapped

I made it to the church, there was no way I'd make it home in time. I'd stay the night. I decided to call Mum, no reply. Suddenly, a door slammed, it sounded like it was from the church. I felt brave enough to investigate.

The door creaked open… *Bang!* The toilet door slammed. I ran to it without hesitation – locked!

I couldn't bear it, but now the front door was locked too!

Then, slowly, the toilet door opened.

'Who's there?' I asked.

There was a cold draught… no windows were open, was it a ghost? I was grabbed…

Joe Churchill Stone (11)

St Birinus School, Didcot

Freddy Fazbear's Pizza

It was a cold night in New York. The wind was blowing and it was drizzling lightly. I was sitting at my desk as always, checking the security scanners, when I saw it. Movement. It was long past closing hours.

I got up from my seat and switched my flashlight on, ready to go and see what was going on...

William Marron

St Birinus School, Didcot

The Ceasefire

Surrounded by decaying bodies and the terrifying sound of warfare, John leaned against the wall of the trench, hoping the ceasefire rumour was true.

His sergeant had ordered the few remaining to clear the trench. John hauled himself and the heavy chest of ammunition up the muddy ruins of the trench wall and he and his mate Albert dragged the chest all the way to the waiting truck. Joking with the driver, they loaded the chest in.

Jubilant and excited to have finally left the trench, they never saw the truck explode, but felt the agony as their lives ended.

Jamie Staples (11)

St Birinus School, Didcot

Fright Night

I was in an abandoned school. A shadow came, but it disappeared. The lights went off. I heard a girl scream. I went to find her. She was chained to a pipe in the bathroom, the door locked, water started dripping from the ceiling. *Drip, drip.*

A snake slithered across my shoe. The floor was filling up. I tried to rescue the girl, but the water was already up to our necks. The lights went off; I couldn't see and I passed out.

When I woke up, I was chained to a car bumper. It started going fast - *boom!*

'Help!'

Kian Lay (11)
St Birinus School, Didcot

Spine-Chiller

I quickly ran down the stairs, something was behind me, it was coming to get me. I quickly barged the door open, I ran into the forest and into the graveyard. I walked over to the door, the doorknob was very rusted. I went inside, there were bats flying in there. One of the bats came flying at me. I ducked.

I called Alfie.

Alfie said, 'I will be there in 20 minutes.'

The shadow was still moving. Something touched me on the shoulder, I turned around and ran back to my house.

JJ got there – I was gone...

Alfie Grisbrooke
St Birinus School, Didcot

Alien Invasion

As the day moved on, The Vamps, the band, were walking down Doom Street. It was windy, the cars were flying. Suddenly, an alien ship arrived, sucking all the humans up that looked at the bright light. The band didn't want to die, so they entered a creepy church, not noticing how creepy it was.

As they entered they weren't really that careful because the alien caught their heads. It walked forward, using its sharp nails, it ripped their throats and turned all of them into zombies.

Emmanuel (11)
St Birinus School, Didcot

They Watch...

It was night, I was in bed looking out of the window that lit yellow from the street light. Then I saw a thin, humanoid-shaped shadow. A round-headed shaped shadow slowly moved to the middle of the window. Then the window smashed, leaving glass all over the floor. Some of the shards were red with blood, but it wasn't mine.

I heard a loud screech as the thin, humanoid figure crawled through the window.

It screeched again as it saw me.

Jamie McMenemy (12)
St Birinus School, Didcot

The House Next Door

The sun lay down and the moon flew up above the dim, black, rotten house next door. The house next door was a daredevil's worst nightmare. No one had been stupid enough to go in there.

I looked out of the window to see a black and foggy air, just before I went, because I wasn't going far. Just up the road to get some groceries.

I could've sworn I'd remembered everything, but obviously not, because I had to go back to get my money.

Suddenly, the door to the house opened, a girl screamed and then I did.

'Aaaargh!

Felix Marsh

St Birinus School, Didcot

Untitled

The dark was falling, the light was going when suddenly all the doors opened. It was someone from the dead...

I called the police, the SWAT team came out and they said someone was targeting me. But they didn't know who.

When I went to the supermarket, I was getting vegetables, then I returned home there was someone again, dead on the floor and there was a man hung up next to him.

I called the police and ambulance to come and investigate. They said they'd committed suicide because of something...

Casey Muldoon (11)

St Birinus School, Didcot

Hidden Danger

'Argh!' she screamed as he plunged a knife into her heart.
One day in the dark woods, two friends were playing hide-and-seek.
The boy's name was Edward, the girl's name was Judy. They were the
best of friends.
In the middle of the game, a dark figure approached, he had a
concealed knife in his cloak. He was an assassin, out to kill Judy (who
was a princess).
He was creeping up on them, they spotted him and ran. When they
turned around, he was gone. They were very scared. He suddenly
popped out of nowhere and cut them down.

Ethan James More O'Ferrall (13)

St Birinus School, Didcot

Always Look In The Shadows

I had just woken, I was still startled. I touched my cold forehead, it
was gushing with blood. I then stood up, the only thing I could see
right now was fog.
Wait! I just saw a gothic-looking character swaying through the fog. I
had to run...
I arrived at a graveyard; I abruptly tripped over. I was knocked
out. I then woke again. The figure I saw in the fog was there. It just
stood there and stared at me with its blood-red, devilish eyes. It then
pounced on me and attacked maliciously.

Samuel Hart (12)

St Birinus School, Didcot

A Halloween Night

It was Halloween night, all the children were out trick or treating, except one and that kid sat in his room alone, with no one else in the house.

He tried to entertain himself, but whatever he did he got bored within two minutes.

Then there was a knock at the door... he opened it and it wasn't trick or treaters, but it was an evil killer. He shut the door and ran. He was terrified.

He went to the bathroom and locked the door, the killer broke in. He knew him, so do you. It was him!

Corey Swaine (12)
St Birinus School, Didcot

Death

One day, a man called Myles Hicks was a survivor and so were John and Steven.

They were all terrified because they were in a zombie apocalypse.

They ran to a different place every day, which, as far as Myles knew, was safe.

There was one guy they knew called Seth, but Seth died. He was eaten alive and it was brutal. All the insides were swallowed by the zombies.

The zombies looked at Myles whilst he was telling the story. He ran and John and Steven were struck. All Myles heard was a brutal scream...

Myles Hicks (12)
St Birinus School, Didcot

Family Reunion

One blustery winter, our family decided to have a Christmas reunion in a huge log cabin in the Alps of Switzerland.
When we arrived we started the celebration by putting the tree up with gorgeous amounts of food and drink.
Suddenly, a tree outside was demolished and destroyed. In the shadows there was a figure of a woman with her face all scabbed up. We could see a big crew of monsters and bears coming towards our house...

Jacob Eamonn Sykes (13)
St Birinus School, Didcot

The Journey Of Death

Ration book in hand, I make my way to the local shop. The short walk always fills me with fear.
Terrified and breathless, I endeavour to think of happy times long ago.
Thoughts of Mother.
Bang! My heart fills with doom.
A familiar noise deafens my ears. A familiar smell fills my nose.
I try to run, but my legs are rooted to the floor, like a 100-year-old tree. I can't run for shelter, I'm sure to die.
My mother's smiling face fills my mind, her long, flowing hair like raven-black silk.
Blacker than death.

Ruby Anna Carty-Din (12)
St George's School, Ascot

Last Moments

'Kiss me,' Penelope rasped shakily, laying her cool hand on the back of my neck.

I gently set it back at her side and did as she asked. Nervous laughter seemed unavoidable. Can't exactly deny a dying woman's request now, can I?

'Damien honey, I'm burning up.'

She coughed weakly, red oozing through the bullet hole in her cobalt-blue dress.

'I-I can't believe... ' I stuttered feeling her forehead and smoothing her strawberry-blonde curls. 'Oh God, stay with me!'

'Shh... ' Penelope whispered, placing a finger to my lips. 'I forgive you... '

Jade Creamer
St Mark's West Essex Catholic School, Harlow

Railway Death

Ella was dead! Her friend Katie was asleep, all of a sudden she had a nightmare.
Her friend, Ella, was a ghost, but instead of being nice, she was evil.
Ella clearly blamed Katie for her death. She thought Katie had pushed her under the train and she was back for revenge.
Ella came rushing at Katie with white, starry eyes and her mouth a black void. She was chanting Katie's name.
Saying, 'You are going to die.'
Katie panicked, she searched the room for a way to escape. Her heart was racing. Her nightmare ended as she woke.

Lucy Denham
St Mark's West Essex Catholic School, Harlow

Sarah's Spirit

There Sarah was, lying in her stone-cold coffin. Millie, her friend, was truly devastated.
'Why must you go?' Millie said sobbing into her cold hands.
Her hair was stuck to her face. Curled into a ball, she began to cry.
Millie decided to make her way home.
Soon after, she felt a small vibration on her left leg. She opened her eyes and... there was Sarah, staring right at Millie. Same brown hair, same clothes, same everything.
'Are you Sarah?' Millie asked shakily.
'I am,' said the spirit calmly.
'Why have you come, I haven't done anything to you!'

Alice Wybrew
St Mark's West Essex Catholic School, Harlow

Black Revenge

I was infatuated by the dark, I loved being in the arms of the black atmosphere that loomed around me. Silence was always at a complete standstill and time always seemed to slow down at this point.

As the nights crept by, the presence of the darkness was becoming a much more familiar surrounding than the day.

Trapped. It's not a word I would've used to describe myself, there and then. Light was my enemy; I had become one with the dreadful black that once swiftly travelled around my inhumanity. Fearless I was, but would fear soon overcome my mind?

Bhavika Makwana (13)
Sarah Bonnell School, London

The Masked Madman

It was the break of midnight, Edward and Ben slowly crept to the abandoned mansion. Apparently, there were mystical creatures which lie there.

As they entered there was creaking and loud bangs on the top floor. Edward was shaking.

Ben stated, 'Don't worry.'

They heard a voice coming from the basement; they decided to go down there. A candle was flickering, there was an outline of four figures. The two boys reached for their cameras.

The men said, 'No pictures.'

A light turned on and the figures were not what they expected...

Connor Gammon (12)
Shirley High School , Croydon

Mummy's Little Boy

One day, at the break of day, a little boy ran across the field that we play in. this little boy would always say, 'Mummy, Mummy, I want to play... '

But no one would play along so, feeling bad, my best friend went down to play with him.

My best friend, Roger, would play with this boy for weeks on end. They played so much that I felt left out. But one day, Roger didn't turn up, so I played with the little boy and I asked him where Roger was.

He replied, deathly, 'Mummy took care of him... '

Chloe Fillon-Payoux (13)

Shirley High School , Croydon

The Meeting

It was a clear but cold night and there was a blanket of stars above me. A glittering frost clung to everything around me. I hoped my mum would remember to meet me on the corner of the street by the cemetery.

I arrived at my destination and already the fog was creeping towards me. I hoped Mum would come soon. The phone in my hand was dead. It made me think about where I was.

'What is that awful smell?'

It seemed to be getting stronger. Panic swelled inside me as two shadows moved in.

'Mum, are you there?'

Andrew Jones (11)

Shirley High School , Croydon

Abduction

It was a cloudy night when a crow landed on a branch outside my bedroom window. A beam of light suddenly hit the ground, pulling me through it! It was as if my body was being stretched.

I woke up in a metal bed with a large, grey-headed creature standing above me. I heard the words, 'Master, he has awoken.'

A scaly being came and touched my chest, making a hole inside it. It then placed a cold, metal object inside me. Just before it let go of the object, a flash of light instantly brought me home.

Curtis Peacock (12)
Shirley High School , Croydon

The Psycho Scientist

'Go to that shut mental asylum, see what's going on, the other five didn't return, also there were noises, complaints from there,' Chief explained.

'No, that place was shut because of the maniacal scientific experiment on people.'

'But we'll be rich,' Chief said.

'Why not?'

So the next day, I cycled to the asylum and when I got there the door was open. I sneaked into the reception and headed inside. There was a computer. I downloaded all the data to my USB. I searched for the mad scientist, then the lights went out.

'You're already dead' the computer typed...

Rojon Yilmaz (12)
Shirley High School , Croydon

The Murder House

The sunlight soon changed to moonlight as Rose approached the old, abandoned house. She felt eyes were upon her, but she just had to investigate the scene of the gruesome murders.

She ducked under the *Keep Out* tape into the darkness. The police never did find their prime suspect. Her heart pounded out of her chest as she saw a menacing figure in a red bomber jacket, holding a knife. She ran.

Later, at home, she rushed towards her dad, but stopped in her tracks and gasped loudly, as he said, 'Oh, don't you like my new red bomber jacket?'

Hannah Bance (12)

Shirley High School , Croydon

The Mask Collection

The twins, Jordan and Josh were getting dinner, killing a pig with their chainsaw in the barn.

They sat down for a rest. There was a ferocious scream that rattled the farm! The boys knew it was their mother.

Three thuds at the door and a strike of lightning...

Jordan shouted, 'The chainsaw, it's gone!'

A man stepped forward, wearing their mother's face.

'Like my mask? I got it from your mother!'

The man chuckled and gutted both the boys like pigs. The man cut the boys' faces off.

His collection of masks had only just begun. He would return!

Jacob Hue (12)

Shirley High School , Croydon

Deathly Hallow

Seeing Mum and Dad in the distance, waving goodbye, made me think, *I'm not that little girl who has tea parties with her dolls. I'm starting a new life on my own.*
I drove closer and closer to the place I'd now be calling home. Driving deeper and deeper into the forest – 99 Lime Road. No, that can't be it. What happened to the house I'd once hoped to call home?
An old ivy-clad house appeared as the fog rolled away. My heart started beating faster, then a hand grabbed my shoulder and pulled me to Death's home.

Abigail Asantewaa (12)
Shirley High School , Croydon

The Abandoned Home

James entered the house. *This is where she said to meet me*, he thought to himself. He shut the door behind him. It was silent, all that could be heard was the thudding of his heart. Then the sound of a window slamming against the frame. He sat down, now he could hear the hoots of an owl. The silence was spine-chilling.
Thud, thud. He heard on the stairs, James sat, frozen. *What could it be?* he thought. Then another thud, but this time it was louder. *Slam!* The door shut as a cold hand touched him…

William Daniels White (12)
Shirley High School , Croydon

The Sleepover

It was a cold, stormy night and Jessica's house was filled with light. Jessica was having a sleepover with her four friends. Everything was so much fun until Mary mentioned to play hide-and-seek. Two were upstairs and one was downstairs, but the counter was not anywhere. Then, suddenly, 'Argh!'
Mary, who was the counter, had been killed. The girls were shocked. All that was heard was a blood-curdling scream and Mary was dead. They were all shocked. Well that's what the rest thought. Jessica gave a bloodthirsty look, everyone had their suspicions...

Omer Sunay Ibrahim (13)

Shirley High School , Croydon

The Wind's Whistle

Today is one heck of a stormy day, I thought to myself. I was trying to get home, but I knew I couldn't get home before nightfall. I stumbled across a building, unidentifiable from all the cracks and ivy on it.
'Hello?' I called, waiting for a response.
Nothing.
'Hello?' I said again, in case they hadn't heard me.
As I went into the building the lights turned off. After some seconds they turned on again. When I took another step, I heard a terrifying scream coming from upstairs! As I got closer, I felt something cold go through me...

Raul Perez Hernandez (12)

Shirley High School , Croydon

The Doll

As the moon created shadows here and there, Lucy and Janice were watching the news. The storm outside gave them quite a scare.

'Three serial killers have escaped and want a doll,' the TV muttered. Lucy saw the doll and flung it at Janice and, with a blink of an eye, it was gone!

As they got ready for bed, they turned and saw the doll lying there, on the bed. The light flickered and then Lucy heard a voice. A cold hand touched her shoulder...

'Janice!'

Splat! Blood squirted everywhere!

Rovita Tambwe (12)

Shirley High School , Croydon

The Basement

One stormy night, two friends were FaceTiming each other. One of the girl's names was Sarah and one's name was Zera. While they were FaceTiming, *bang!* A noise came from the basement at Sarah's.

'What was that?' shouted Sarah.

'I dare you to check it out,' said Zera.

'No way, I'm not that brave,' said Sarah.

'You're a mouse,' laughed Zera to Sarah.

'OK, OK, I will check it out, but only if you stay online with me.'

'OK,' said Zera.

So Sarah went down. Suddenly Zera shrieked.

'What is this, I'm sorry I dared you!'

Eren Aziz Aray (12)

Shirley High School , Croydon

Demons

She was standing there, holding my parents' heads, towering over their dead bodies! Her long golden hair turned black, her face turned pale with dark marks circling her eyes. Lights were dim and flickering, the windows were smashing against the frames as the wind howled. Rain flooded into the house, lightning struck and the house went pitch-black.

The wooden floorboards started creaking, I felt my little sister grasping my leg. Fast steps got louder... there was a breathtaking scream which echoed. The lights came on and a bloody knife dropped to the floor. Then she came...

Amirah Tahir (12)

Shirley High School , Croydon

Dawn Of The Decorations

It was a dark night and Chloe was getting ready for bed. Her parents were away all weekend, so she was alone.

Bang! Chloe jumped out of her skin. *Boom!* The noise came from the loft! Being her normal adventurous self, Chloe went to look. She heard a scuttle from the Christmas box. Suddenly her torch flickered on and off, on and off till it stopped and the only light left was from a hole in the roof.

As she turned around to lift the box, her torch turned on, but another voice spoke and a shadow appeared...

Lauren Wills (12)

Shirley High School , Croydon

The Last Footstep

Running, sprinting, Renn scrambled all over the place, trying to get away from the dangerous bear. Her legs started to betray her. Every breath she took would become a drop from her soul into fear. 'Sophia,' whispered Renn as she took deep breaths. 'Help Sophia!' As she turned around, the sky became pitch-black. No one to be seen. No one to be heard. No one to survive.

Renn heard a twitch from a tree branch, a cold, furry hand touched her shoulder. The last words to come out were, 'Renn this is your last chance to live... '

Shamoy Chenel Simmonds (11)
Shirley High School , Croydon

Untitled

In a cold, freezing house, where a family was huddled up, Mum was cooking with the family, waiting for their TV show. A little girl was upstairs, playing with dolls. She found another doll in her wardrobe. The door suddenly shut quickly!

The next day, she checked with her friends at school, but it wasn't theirs. She went home still thinking about it.

When she got home, she looked in the bag for it. There was a note saying: 'Come downstairs to the basement'. So she did and walked inside to the doll - the door shut and locked...

Leah Palmer (13)
Shirley High School , Croydon

Stockholm Syndrome

I woke up in hospital; I knew I was dying and that I loved him. I'd rather bail the ocean from the Earth than see him behind bars. I'd rather stay captive myself than see 'them'. I saw 'them' at the police station, dripping with concern – drowning. My family. It made me sick, I only wanted him.

They said he had kidnapped me; that last week I'd let him feed me something laced with poison. It had burnt up my heart, the doctors said. I shrugged, it had tasted good. All that warmth inside me had tasted like love.

Megan Massey (16)
The Bedford Sixth Form, Bedford

Monsters Of The Mind

I curl in my bed facing the wall... afraid. There's nothing to be afraid of they say - but then again, they didn't see it. Most adults didn't. Notice the feeling of being watched: it's not a mind trick. There every night, when you hear the whistling of the wind and the tapping sound on your window. When shadows dance in the corner of your eyes, you cower under the bed sheets.

When you tell yourself many times it's not real - when in truth, you know the reality of these childhood fears...

Melike Ozzengin (14)
The Urswick School, London

Shadow

It slithers along beside you, tracing your path – a silhouette of a lost soul, devouring every flicker of life within you. It grows so high, only to shrink back. It longs to be observed, be aided and be loved. It treasures your dread and embraces your fear.

Sometimes, when a person allows it to torment them so much, they change. They turn wretched, perplexed and hateful. They suppress everyone who cares for them and become so beat-up, that one day... they are gone.

Nothing but a silhouette who traces your path... never noticed. Always there.

Molly Francesca Ferris (11)

Wallingford School, Wallingford

Darkness!

As the night unwrapped itself, my mind was like a jigsaw. It felt like my brain was dead.

I found a house in the woods, I couldn't contain myself. I just had to go in. I knocked to see if someone was in, but no one was there. I opened the creaky door, it was an old mansion. There was a mirror on the wall with writing on it. It said, 'You're not alone, you're mine now'.

I thought I saw someone behind me, but no one was there. Every time I looked in the mirror, I looked dead...

Bethan Richie (12)

Wood Green School, Witney

The Deserted School

I had just finished my detention, on my way out of the building I heard a creak coming from the door. I said to myself, 'It's just the wind.'
Then I realised that it was darker than usual, which seemed odd.
I carried on through the school and then I thought, *am I actually alone?*
I saw a light flicker in the distance and my maths teacher walked out of the room with an evil look on her face. Then, all of a sudden, a vicious shadow appeared there...

Blaine Eason (12)
Wood Green School, Witney

A Day In The Graveyard

I am in a graveyard, playing hide-and-seek. The trees start to rustle loudly. I look around, then it stops. I turned back to see my grandad's grave, the noise started again, so I leave. Then it gets louder.
I hear a big 'Help!'
I go to see, and all there is, is a blood trail leading into a church. I go in, but it stops at the doors. I go back to my grandad's grave and all the other graves have gone!
The doors are locked and my grandad's grave is gone too!

Graeme Bateman (12)
Wood Green School, Witney

The Eyes In The Corner

It was dark when I saw it. Crimson mysteries hidden within ghostly, white eyes. All I saw was his eyes and his body looked nothing more than a jet-black mass, hidden in a midnight alley. He suited the alley, skulking in a corner. Black smears of paint, resembling words that couldn't be said aloud, rust eating at the bricks like a ravenous lion. When the figure saw me, he fell, limp, like a puppet, clinging against the cracking walls; I walked on. Turning back, the figure had gone.

Meagan Brien (13)
Wood Green School, Witney

The Porcelain Masks

I'm drowning in the masks. Porcelain faces with blank expressions, haunted and in pain. Millions of mortified faces drown me. I search for myself in them, wading through them as they stare at me in distaste. Past personalities shattered and frozen in china, their dying expressions staring.
Above me is a lifeless abyss of endless black, the stars shining pinpricks that dwell in the souless sky. I sink into the faces beneath my feet and they drag me into the depths. I feel my pained expression setting into my face in a pearly mask as I am split from reality…

Kayleigh Gardikioti-Griva (12)
Wood Green School, Witney

Young Writers
Est.1991

YOUNG WRITERS
INFORMATION

We hope you have enjoyed reading this book – and that you will continue to in the coming years.

If you're a young writer who enjoys reading and creative writing, or the parent of an enthusiastic poet or story writer, do visit our website www.youngwriters.co.uk. Here you will find free competitions, workshops and games, as well as recommended reads, a poetry glossary and our blog.

If you would like to order further copies of this book, or any of our other titles, then please give us a call or visit **www.youngwriters.co.uk.**

Young Writers
Remus House
Coltsfoot Drive
Peterborough
PE2 9BF
(01733) 890066 / 898110
info@youngwriters.co.uk